THE STORY

OF

SADIE FOX

Based on a True Story

MARTHA PEREZ

The Story of Sadie Fox

© 2018 by Martha Perez

ISBN: 978-0-9998843-5-5

For more information or to book an event,
contact Martha Perez or Sal Andalon

memartha@ymail.com
salandalon@ymail.com
or visit www.marthaperez.info

Cover Design by The Book Khaleesi

TABLE OF CONTENTS

PROLOGUE

I stare out the window of my small apartment. I don't step outdoors anymore. All I do is watch the people and the kids outside my living room window. There's something to be said for watching people living their lives; kids laughing, their moms and dads holding hands, taking care of their children. How I envy those people. I'm sitting in my coziest recliner. It's very comfy... and I look around at the four walls that seem to be closing in on me. I'm not that typical young woman any longer. So much has happened to me. I've tried to walk outside but as soon I'm at the front door... my knees start to wobble and then I start quivering. I just can't be around people. I feel dazed, isolated, and out of control.

I only have one child and my husband had left

me for a younger woman. I gave my whole heart to that man, even when it wasn't his to take. He took my heart, really, I didn't give it to him at all and he stole everything I had. He just took it and sold it to his friends. They say love is blind and it's the truth, so help me God. My life has been rough around the edges and so tough. You feel a numbness—the pain in my heart, as if someone is twisting a knife – from the ache that I feel. I was innocent once. A person can break you and smash your heart, your body, and your soul, to smithereens, along with all your hopes and dreams. Yet, somehow, you can't live without that person. Love is not about pain, hurt, fear, or even feeling damaged. It's about respecting yourself, being kind to yourself, making yourself number one and laughing at the smallest things, holding hands, making love. You know what I mean... the hearts and flowers kind of things you hear about, what you read about. The 'happy ever after' in books. Well... that wasn't my life.

My world was about drinking, sex, getting beaten up when I never even deserved it, getting fucked and passed around like a whore.

Yeah, life wasn't what I'd expected at all. Your heart wants what it shouldn't want. How easy was it to walk away? Fear got in the way – the key to my heart wasn't his to hold. He could easily destroy it and he did. What I'm talking about is my husband never made love to me, never loved me. Instead, he passed me around his group of poker buddies. That's exactly what he did and he damaged me to the point of no return. But yet I loved him and did things that I shouldn't have done. Will that never change?

Chapter 1

SADIE

I'd just turned sixteen, with straight, long, blonde hair, staring at the mirror, my huge diamond-blue eyes sparkling, my lips thick and rosy. I put on tons of lip gloss. I have porcelain fair skin and my body certainly has curves. I already have double 'D' breasts and a small waist. I'm innocent and still a virgin. While some of my friends at school are having sex, I want to hold on to my virginity until I finish school and get married. That's my dream... someday, shortly. They say you have to watch out what you wish for.

5

MARTHA PEREZ

I'm an only child, living in a two-story house, with a white picket fence, in Los Angeles, our home; not a safe area. Mama was very strict. She told me, all the time, if I ever had sex or got pregnant, she would not let me live in her home. I always did what Mama said. My Dad passed away before I was born and Mama remarried. Her new husband was a quiet man; Mama controls him and everything around her. I never called him Daddy, but always just by his name, Troy, Troy Mills. I didn't take his last name because that's the way Mama wanted it. Troy loved me so much; he would help me with my homework and give me hugs, just like a normal Dad would do. Mama gave me kisses and hugs, always showing me love. She taught me how to bake and she loved making all my clothes for me. Mama is a large woman but she's beautiful. She has blue eyes and straight blonde hair. Troy was almost bald and the little hair he did have was salt and pepper colored. He had a light complexion, with his body tending more on the thinner side.

"Mama, could Dottie come over, please? We have a test to study for," I asked.

"If it's for studying, okay, no problem," she replied.

Mama was always fair and let me basically do whatever I wanted to do, but you would never cross Mama. As long you did what was expected and required, she'd just leave you alone. Her baking is to die for. Dottie loves eating at my house because it's all always comfort food. Mama bakes cookies for Dottie and me to eat on my bed. We're laughing and joking around. Dottie is my best friend, who I've known since kindergarten. She is a beautiful girl, with dark, short, wavy hair, green emerald eyes, and a gorgeous tan. She's thin, without big breasts like me, and she always says how jealous she is of mine.

"God, Sadie, I want those huge tits."

"Dottie! Shut up! They're called breasts."

She rolls her eyes and we both giggle. Dottie

looks around the room. "You got new picture frames and a comforter."

"Yeah, Mama said it was time for a change," I reply.

"You're so lucky. My mom doesn't change them until you can see through them." Dottie gives another silly laugh.

My room is nice; it's painted pink and my pictures on the wall are flowers, all different kinds since I'm crazy about flowers. My comforter is covered in flowers, also.

Dottie talks about her new boyfriend. Dale Coleman is cute, with huge, dark chocolate eyes. He works out, so you can imagine how he rocks the bad-boy look and at six-feet tall, he even has sculpted abs and those lips of his give me goosebumps just thinking about them.

"Boy, you have it bad for him, Dottie," I note.

"Going to tell you a secret, Sadie. I had sex with him," she responds.

I put my cookie down quickly. "How was it?

Was he sweet with you? Did it hurt? Come on, spill, Dot." I wanted to know, since I'd never had sex and Dottie was the same age as me. She has slept around before and I just feel she's too young for that. She should be enjoying her adolescence. Dottie gives me a mischievous grin. I just stare at her. "Well, you going to spill or not?"

I start to eat my cookie again, since Dottie is taking so long to answer, then she blurts out, "He has a huge penis!"

I start choking, so badly I spit my cookie on Dottie's face. We both start chuckling, our giggles becoming earsplitting. We eat our cookies in silence, for a moment, drinking our milk as we continue our girl talk. It was too interesting not to talk about Dottie's love life at sixteen years of age.

"You know, Sadie, he has a friend and I told him about you," Dottie says.

"NO! Thanks, Dottie, I won't be set up with any guy, come on!" I argue.

"He wants to meet you."

9

"No!" I exclaim vehemently. "I can certainly find my own boyfriend and I will not have sex until I get married. You don't have to have sex with a guy you just met. Maybe you will like him if he's older. It's kind of terrifying, actually. They're men already and they expect so much more, but we're too young for them. I want to be a teenager still and not to grow up faster than we should."

Dottie smirks. "Just meet him, please! For me, come on, Sadie," she begs.

"I'll think about it, for sure, okay?"

Dottie goes home.

"Sadie, are you in bed yet?" Mama calls.

"Yes, Mama!"

"Good night then. Don't let the bedbugs bite or something to that effect," she mumbles.

She's been saying that ever since I was five and I never got why she told me that, as we currently don't have bed bugs, or ever, as far as I know.

THE STORY OF SADIE FOX

Lying on my bed, thinking about what Dottie had said, not knowing why it bothered me so much. Shaking my head, I ended up tossing and turning all night, in a relatively sleepless night. I woke up in not so much of a great mood, not helped by taking a cold shower.

"Mama! The water is cold!" I holler.

"Sorry Sadie," is all she could offer. Troy, though, realizes what's wrong with my body feeling like a block of ice, getting my pink towel for me. Shivering like I lived at the North Pole and running through the hallway with my pink terry robe to my room. There is nothing worse than taking a cold shower.

I'm wearing my new skinny jeans with a new pullover sweater and yes, it has flowers on it, but it is so warm. I put my blonde hair into a ponytail.

Troy calls out, "Honey, are you ready?"

"Sure am!" I respond eagerly.

On my way to school, Troy always takes me to a donut shop for hot chocolate and a glazed donut, my favorite; that was the highlight of my day. He parks in front of the school.

"See you later, Sadie. You want me to pick you up after school?"

"No, I want to walk today, but thanks." He kisses my cheek.

Running to my class, Dottie is grinning like the cat that ate the canary. "Sadie, he wants to meet you."

"Who?"

"Dale's friend, Drake Fox."

"Oh, I don't know about that, Dottie."

"He's charming, Sadie. We'll go on a double date so that you won't be alone with him at any time. So, what do you say?"

"Alright, just never leave me alone with him, okay?"

"Gotcha!" Dottie grins.

"Okay girl, got to go. Bye, Dot."

"I'll tell you later what time on Saturday evening we're going to the movies," she throws at me as I leave.

*   *   *

"Mama! I'm home!"

"Hi, dear. Do your homework, now."

"Okay, Mama."

Lying on my bed, doing my homework, Dottie calls me. "What's up, girl?"

"We're going to the movies at six, so look your best – and Sadie, don't act like you're scared, alright?" Dottie begs.

"Okay, Dot, I won't."

*   *   *

"Mama, just to let you know, on Saturday I'll be going to the movies with Dottie."

"What time, Sadie?" Mama asks.

"Six."

"Why so late?"

"Because that's when the movie is showing, Mama, okay?"

"Don't be home too late," she insists.

"Okay, Mama."

Troy comments that it's overly late for me to be going to the movies.

"Don't worry, Troy, she's fine and I trust my daughter."

"Well, if you say so. She's a beautiful girl and I just don't want some asshole to take advantage of her," Troy responds.

"You worry too much, old man." Mama smiles at him.

I am so nervous about the date with Drake, feeling so uneasy that he's older than me. What if he wants to touch me? Guys like that can't be trusted, right? Or am I just over-analyzing the whole matter? Hopefully, he's a nice guy like Dottie says and not just an asshole trying to get himself a piece of ass.

THE STORY OF SADIE FOX

*   *   *

Friday, going to class, Dottie bumps arms with me. "Hi, Sadie! Can't wait for you to meet Dale."

"Is that all you think about, Dot?"

"I'm just excited for us, girl. I know you better than you think. Quit thinking, girl. It's just a date, not a lifetime commitment, or forever, for God's sake."

Chapter 2

SADIE

Today is Saturday – a new day, the important date. I'm going to meet Drake Fox. I don't know what the fuss is all about. I'm very uneasy. I have a whole room full of clothes but have no idea what to wear and anyway, why do I care what he would think? My final choice was simple skinny jeans and the baby pink t-shirt with a darker pink sweater, some black flat boots, with my blonde, straight, silky hair flowing down. I'm wearing my shirt so my large breasts won't stand out – they are massive! I only hope he likes me for me and not for my breasts. I wear a matching pink cotton bra and cotton bikini panties, some light makeup, pink lipstick, and I'm already waiting for Dottie. I go downstairs, where Troy is watching television.

"Sadie, you look beautiful," he greets me.

"Thanks." I smile shyly.

"Sit next to me, please, Sadie. Guys are naïve when it comes to girls. They don't think with their brains, and remember what your Mama said... if it gets nasty with a boy, she won't let you come back home. So, be careful."

I know he means well. "I'll be okay, Troy, promise." I kiss his cheek as I hear a honk.

"Dottie's here," Mama calls.

"Bye, Mama!"

Running down the short driveway to where Dottie is opening the car door, I slide in. Dale shyly says hi to me and I respond in kind. Dottie wasn't kidding. He's handsome with a 'sugar and spice and everything nice' bad-boy look. He's wearing black jeans paired with a black t-shirt with a dragon decal in the center, his muscles bulging out. I don't stare long at him, but still, he smirks, with a sly grin, more like a cocky one, I think.

"Sadie, Drake is meeting us there," Dottie tells me.

"That's fine," I respond.

I'm thankful that Dottie is wearing skinny jeans like mine. Her brown, wavy hair is between Dale's fingers, pulling her straight to him. Staring out the window, I marvel at the car. It's kinda an expensive Bentley; it's new, with all black, tinted windows and black leather seats.

When we arrive at the movie theater, Dale and Dottie go in and tell me to wait right there. So here I am, freezing my ass off, for a guy no less.

*   *   *

DRAKE

Drake watches her from afar, her silky blonde hair swaying in front of her face.

She seemed cold but what got my attention was her breasts. They're huge! She's also curvy, in all the right places. Fuck! She's making my dick stiff already. I adjust my huge pole and remind myself that this girl is young and just the right age for my appetite. She will be mine tonight! I have big plans for her. Too bad Sadie has no idea her life is about to change forever.

Walking straight to her, I realize she's even more beautiful up close.

"Are you Sadie?" I ask, making my voice as sexy as I can, and with my seductive grin, she's blushing, all so cute and young. She's so damn sweet, but hell, I can't stop glancing at her tits. I'm that guy mothers fear. I don't look like a bad boy, no tattoos, and I'm a smooth talker, but, damn, I want to touch her like right now. Got to control my thoughts.

"Yes, I'm Sadie," she responds, her cheeks all rosiness. "Are you Drake?"

"In the flesh." I give her my sexiest smile this time. "Let's go inside. You seem like you're cold?"

Noticing her nipples are hard, I want to bite them until she screams my name. Wow! Sometimes I wish my mind could get out of the gutter for at least a few hours or maybe one, anyway. "Sadie, would you like some popcorn or Coke? How about some candy?"

"Yes please," she answers, smiling.

She's so adorable. That's my kind of girl.

We watch the movie and it's the most boring chick-flick I've ever seen. Getting more annoyed by the minute, my hand is sliding up her thigh and she tenses.

"Relax, sweet girl. This is the reason couples come to the movies; to mess around."

She relaxes again.

*   *   *

SADIE

He's gorgeous, this guy; with those brown, slanted eyes that sparkle, with fair skin, maybe six-feet tall, thick red lips, jet black hair pulled back with gel and his scent of expensive cologne. His smell is divine, still too much for me, and he has nice muscles. He's wearing a black sweater, with black slacks. Drake is older, that's for sure. What he wants with a sixteen-year-old is what's bugging me the most.

Drake starts to kiss my neck, licking in smooth, long licks with his tongue. He whispers, "Relax," then he turns my face and kisses my full lips. This is all new to me, so I let him continue. I've never been kissed or touched like this. He starts to feel my breasts and pinches one of my nipples. It feels kinda good.

"You like me touching your breasts and you're going to be a good girl and let me slurp them," he whispers in the darkness.

I start to protest, but he shuts me down. "Shhhh! Just let me suck them and show you a great time."

"I haven't let anyone touch me before," I say.

"Shhhh! Baby, don't talk, just feel."

I'm getting in way over my head. Where are Dottie and Dale? They're doing exactly what we're doing – messing around.

"I want to go home, please," I finally manage to squeeze out.

"Come on, baby, you like what I'm doing to you."

"I want to go home!" I stand up to walk away when Drake grabs my arm firmly.

"I'll take you home," he grits between his teeth.

"Thank you," I gratefully respond.

We walk to the Bentley, but why?

"Are you taking Dale's car?" I ask.

*   *   *

DRAKE

"It's mine, sweet girl, let's get you home." I smirk. Yeah, right, she's never going home.

"You're going the wrong way, Drake," Sadie squeaks.

"Just want to show you where I live," I reply.

I watch her from the corner of my eye. She's scared and for good reason. I take what I want and tonight, I want her. I'll fuck her the way I want and no one will stop me. I know, I'm an awful jerk, always have been and always will be.

*   *   *

SADIE

MARTHA PEREZ

Drake parked the car in front of a house, telling me it had three bedrooms. I just nodded my head, like I should even care. If I had taken the time to notice, I would have seen the house was on a little hill, with no neighbors. The house is modern and light with lots of large palm trees and lovely white window frames. The windows have a dark tint to them. As far as I can tell, the property was nice, with well-trimmed lawns. He holds my hand and unlocks the expensive, ivory front door.

Inside was not what I expected, with clean smells like a nice, sweet candy scent. We walked to the front room, which boasted two dark-blue leather couches, a recliner, and an enormous flat-screen television. In the dining room stood a poker table, with six chairs, two lamps on each side, and a huge bar with all kinds of liquor bottles of every variety. The walls were covered in picture frames of girls in bikinis, so typical for a guy's house.

"Sadie, let's go to the kitchen and get something to drink."

I reluctantly tag along behind him.

"So what do you think about my house?"

"It's nice, Drake, really beautiful."

"You're the one that's beautiful, Sadie." His thumb runs down my cheek. "What would you like to drink, sweet girl?"

"Any kinda soda would be great if you have any," I responded.

His kitchen is medium size, with a glass table, six chairs, fridge, and a stove. They all look brand new. Two windows, cloaked in dark, navy-blue curtains, make everything seem dark and expensive.

*   *   *

DRAKE

I'm pouring her a cherry Coke with two pills dissolved in it. I need her to relax. I still want her to feel every inch of my cock when I slide it in. Oh sure, she'll hurt, but I'm a cocky son-of-a-bitch and if I'm right that she's a virgin, then she definitely needs some loosening up. I'm feeling my cock stir just thinking about it. I don't really like popping cherries, but Sadie's different, she's my money maker. She'll pay my debts! Like I said, I'm an asshole, cocky bastard, so I got to focus on my game.

"Come on, sweet girl, let's have a seat." She's getting nervous. "Drink your Coke, there's a good girl."

She takes a huge drink. That's my girl. It's going to be kicking in real quick. We start to talk, then she says she has to go home.

All I tell her is, "You got some time, don't worry, Sadie, trust me."

I could already see her relaxing, with that sweet smile that tells me she doesn't want to hurt my feelings. Sadie is now yawning, my cue.

"Come here, baby." I grin at her.

"I'm so tired, Drake. Please take me home. My Mama won't let me back in my house if I don't come home soon."

Quickly, I pull her into my arms and take her to my bedroom. She's drowsy now, just the way I want. Sadie will be this way all night, so I get my black sweater and shirt off and my pants, hoping she approves of my six-pack and, of course, my long and thick pole. Yeah, I know I'm bragging, because Sadie will soon slurp my penis. I want her to be a good slut and a great screw. So that if I lose to my poker buddies, she'll be sucking their dicks and have sex with them, to satisfy my debts. Believe me, after I'm through with Sadie, she will be the biggest slut you have ever seen.

I remove Sadie's pink t-shirt and gaze at the

lovely sight that greets me. Even in her cotton pink bra, those tits are bursting out, so beautiful, so firm. Removing her pants straight off along with those pink, cotton panties, I realized I'd never thought of cotton as being particularly sexy, but with Sadie wearing it, shit, it looks sexy on her. Her huge breasts and small waist, with curvy thighs that would rock any man's world, just heighten my desire. I can't wait to put my tongue on the soft, blonde curls of her pink pussy and the rest of her smoking-hot body so I could lick her clean. Once again, my dick twitches. It has a mind of its own, you dirty, nasty penis. Sadie mumbles that she wants to go home.

"Shhhhh! Sweet girl, you're going to feel so good."

I grab a handful of her hair and pull her mouth to me forcefully, sticking my tongue down deeper. Her eyes are glazed and she even moans. Pulling her hair back to expose her neck and licking her throat, I suck one of her areolas, sucking it so brutally. I can't help myself, while her moans are getting loader. Fuck! She likes it rough, does she? Putting my whole face between her huge tits, I grab both, squeezing them together and licking both breasts at the same time. Rubbing her sweet muff with my finger, making small circles, I slide one finger into her pussy. She's so wet that I stick two fingers in. Her moans and groans are going to make me blow my load. *I'm going to make you cum, sweet girl.* I grin to myself. Swirling my tongue in her muffin, real deep, licking faster and tasting her nectar, with her sweet scent of peaches, is making me senseless as hell. I feel her legs buck and she yells my name.

"Drake! Ohhhh!"

"That's right, sweet girl! You can cum all over my tongue," I encourage her. She's still mumbling some shit about home. It's time for my sweet fill-up girl. I roll a condom with lubricant and open her legs. My huge cock opens her pussy lips and I push down hard. She screams so loud, grabbing her hair tightly.

"Shut the hell up, bitch!" Her tears are running down her soft cheeks as I slam my pole home. My release is such an intense fuck. "Girl, I'm just going to screw you, again and again. Get used to it." I go to the bathroom, dispose of the condom, get a small towel, wet it with warm water and wipe her sweet little love button. I'm not a total jerk; got to clean her up, because my penis wants her again. Sadie's still in a daze, she's hurting and mumbling about home.

"You're not going home, sweetheart. You're mine to do what I please with, so shut the hell up, I'm not finished with you yet! Do what I say and things will go smoothly. If not, well, I'll just punish you." Yanking her hair, I know she understands when she moans, nodding her head. "Yeah, that's right, you'll be feeling good when my steel pole slips up your sweet muff again."

I want her to be ready soon. My need for her and the money she'll be making for me at my next poker game means I need to teach her some things.

"Touch your tits, Sadie. Do it now!" She gets scared and she starts to put her small hand on her huge breasts. "Yeah, massage them, pinch your nipples. That's right, baby, put your other hand on your muffin and rub your fingers inside your pussy – that's it."

She says my name, "Drake," like a sweet song. I just watch her. I'm hard as a rock and turning her around I tell her I'm soon going to have sex with that backside.

"I'm an ass guy, so I'll get you ready for that." I put my finger between her cheeks and she tenses up big time. "Relax, Sadie," I reassure her. Tearing the package of condoms with my teeth, I put one on and slam my penis into her backside. Wow, it's tight! She yells and screams like the devil. Dang, her cries are so loud they make me want to slam her harder. Yeah! I get off on it, so sue me. I'm the devil, if you want to call me that. So what, she's mine now. I'm a sex-addicted monster.

I let her rest for an hour but I just can't get enough of her. I want to tie her up because I'm a kinky son of a bitch. I have some handcuffs and begin putting them on her wrists. Sadie is still naked and still smelling like sex. She must have had five orgasms already and my dick is getting harder again by the minute. I want her to slurp my pole. "Open your mouth, Sadie," I command. She's still in a daze and when she opens her eyes, the tears are flowing. I shove my penis into her mouth and she starts to gag, so I sit her up. "Start working it, girl, or I'll do nasty things to that backside again." Boy, she didn't think twice before she starts to suck real hard. All the sounds she makes are driving me so fucking crazy. She's gagging because I'm a greedy man and I shove my penis all the way down her throat. I burst my stickiness and she starts to choke on it, but she manages to swallow half my cream down her throat. That's my good, sweet girl. Turning her around I start slapping her backside hard, so hard she screams bloody murder. Sorry, sweet girl, but I love your screams. They only turn me on more. I uncuff her, letting her sleep for two hours.

It's four in the morning now and I'm squeezing her breasts. I know they're sensitive, but I don't care. Knowing for a fact her pussy is throbbing, as well as that ass of hers, makes me pleased.

"Drake, they're sore," she begs.

"Quiet, or I'll punish you, Sadie. I told you I was fucking you all night, didn't I?"

Yeah, she was still groggy, so the sleaze that I am, with my hand covering her mouth, I sealed off her cries and fucked her one more time.

Chapter 3

SADIE

The next morning was the biggest nightmare of all. I can't believe Drake drugged me and raped me. I opened my eyes and he was next to me, his leg around mine. Wanting to vomit so badly, I realize there's stickiness all over my face and the sheets were bloody where he took my virginity. Lips trembling, trying not to weep and scream at the same time, this is what nightmares are made of. Why me?

Getting up, Drake stops me. "Where do you think you're going?" he demands.

With a whisper, I answer, "Bathroom."

"You go when I say you can go. Come here and do your thing, then go take a shower. We're going to Vegas to get married because you belong to me now. Your Mama told Dottie she doesn't want you because you're a dirty girl. Now start slurping!"

My hands are trembling.

"Put your sweet muffin on my face. I'll lick that sweet muff and you can suck my dick with your soft lips. Open your mouth, Sadie, real wide. I have a huge steel pole so go deep, lick the tip, and stop gagging, or I'll spank your ass again and this time it'll be with my belt."

*   *   *

DRAKE

Poor, sweet Sadie. Training has been such fun. I know the poker guys like rough sex; they're kinky sons-of-bitches. She obeys so beautifully. "Yeah, that's it!" I encourage. I start to lick and suck her pink pussy. I know she's so sore and I suck even faster. "Oh, yeah! Oh, yeah! You like my penis, girl. Suck harder – shit, don't bite it, girl. You're asking for that belt, aren't you?" Yanking her hair, I scream in her face, "Don't FUCKING bite, Sadie." Throwing her on top of the bed, I rip another condom, suck her tits once more, and then slam into her pink pussy, so hard. This time her cries are silent, then she says my name and we both have an orgasm. That's my girl, you learn fast.

*   *   *

SADIE

I could scarcely walk with my soreness. Even my jaw hurt... my entire body was in pain. Walking slowly toward the shower, feeling filthy and then letting the water spray my sore, used body, holding my face and wanting to scream bloody murder, I fell down against the tile wall, weeping so quietly. I will never be the same. Was Dottie in on this game of rape? Why me? Why did this happen to me? Washing myself raw, forcing myself to get out of the shower, I note he has clothes for me laid out on top of his bed. A simple white, short dress made out of silk, and white heels.

*   *   *

Drake and I are at the cheapest Wedding Chapel money could buy. Elvis is marrying us and all this feels like a nightmare that I'm praying I'm going to wake up from, any minute now, or maybe the nightmare is just beginning and this is the start of my horrendous new life. Drake stares at me. He's so gorgeous and sweet-looking. You wouldn't think he could do what he did, but he did rape me and now he's looking like he is truly a great guy and he's fooling everyone. Not paying attention, I realize Elvis said, "Now, you're husband and wife, Mr. and Mrs. Fox."

Drake is wearing a black suit; he loosens his tie and gives me a chaste kiss, before he whispers in my ear, "Sadie Fox, you're mine now. Let's celebrate. We have a night at the motel."

The cheap motel that seems dirty, as I look around.

"Come here, Sadie. Now that you're my wife you are going to do whatever I ask, whenever I ask it. Tonight we're going to fuck and you will do everything I ask."

I just want to die. I'm so sore from last night.

"What I want, Sadie, is for you to take that dress off."

I am wearing a white lace thong and a white lace shelf bra. He hands me a glass of beer and puts a pill into it.

"This will relax you. Don't you want to please your husband, Sadie?" he murmurs, with a low voice. "Yes, that's my little slut."

Drake wanted me in a mood of lust, so he makes me watch porn first. "Drink up," he demands.

I focus on watching this movie. I'm so confused by it; two guys are fucking the same girl. Drinking some more beer, I watch as one guy has sex with her from behind and the other from the front. Drake opens another can of beer and pours me more, then has a seat beside me where I'm watching the movie.

I'm getting wet and horny and I've never felt these kind of feelings before. The girl in the movie is yelling, "Yes, fuck! Yes, fuck me."

*   *   *

DRAKE

I glance over and notice Sadie's cheeks are

flushed. "Come over here, Sadie, and sit on my lap, facing me." I start off feeling her huge breasts, licking, sucking, playing with them and teasing them firmly, very harshly, in fact. My steel pole wants to burst but I won't, though. Sadie is so hot. I throw her on top of the bed, put some oil shit all over her pussy and behind. I put my finger in her backside as my other hand squeezes one of her tits. Damn girl, you're so hot and you want my big penis. "Tell me, Sadie. Ask me to fuck you hard." She's too embarrassed to tell me, though. "Stop being so skittish, or do you want me to punish you again? Say it!" I grab both her arms and shake her. "Say it, damn you!"

With embarrassment and in a quiet voice, she says, "Fuck me hard, Drake."

"You bet I'm going to fuck you roughly, sweet girl." Making her watch more porn, I even make her copy the girls in the movie. I take her into the shower and make her suck my cock. Massaging my back, I decide to be nice to her and rub soap all over her huge tits, because it's our wedding night and all. Like I've always said, I'm an arrogant and egotistical ass.

I let Sadie rest. She's exhausted. I'm talking with my brother, Calvin. "Yes, I got married, bro. She's sixteen. We're coming home, Cal, and you're going to take care of her for a week. I got a poker tournament to go to. I trust you, that's why. Yeah, whatever, just do it! She's my ticket, yes. I already popped her cherry, so she's hot, bro, yeah! Be there soon."

*   *   *

Dottie had brought all her clothes as her Mama wanted nothing to do with Sadie, being upset, I guess. That will be in my favor, believe me. Sadie shyly asks to take a shower. I tell her to go, we will stop and eat, then go home. We go to a fast food restaurant. Poor girl, she was starving judging from the way she devoured the meal. I wished I could feel sorry for her, but can't do it – gotta be this way because she'll be the slut of my house. When my buddies and Calvin see her and they know I don't do relationships, they will want to have sex with her, that's for sure, and I'll just be the guy sharing my wife.

Her mother didn't waste any time signing the papers so I could marry Sadie. Everything is legal.

"Wake up, Sadie, my steel pole is throbbing for you." Her eyelids are heavy, trying to open up. I'm saying, "Girl, my cock is excruciating!" Her hands fumble pulling down my zipper. I'm still driving as her soft hands hold my junk and then her mouth's licking it, with her tongue swishing up and down. "That's right, baby, you're a good little wife, sweet girl. Deeper, yeah, almost there." She sucks harder and my cream goes down her throat, so she has my cream running down her chin. "Get some napkins and clean your mouth, girl. Drink a soda, my beautiful adorable girl. I love that you obey me." Then I yank a handful of her hair, kissing those full, swollen lips.

*　　*　　*

SADIE

I just can't believe he can want sex so much. I'm so tired and so sore. This is too much and I simply don't know what to do. I'm a sex-slave, a slut, a whore, and I just want to collapse, sleep forever.

The drive is long and at least he lets me sleep for a while, dreaming I'm at home, happy with Mama and Troy, my room, but then Drake wakes me up. We're home – he calls it home, I call it a sex-slave residence. Drake opens the door and my whole body aches so badly it almost felt like a two-mile walk, just taking a few steps. I take a blessed nap after Drake lets me into one of the bedrooms, while he's talking to Calvin in the kitchen.

"Drake, why did you get a girl that's sixteen?" Calvin asks. "Sadie doesn't look like it, though, she looks more like eighteen, but that's still young, even for you, bro."

"Calvin, after you see what she can do, you won't care what age she is."

"Drake, I'm really more into girls that are at least eighteen."

Drake rolls his eyes. "Yeah, sure you are."

I almost forgot where I am, or that I'm married to a sex-addicted Drake Fox. I stare at the window. It's dark, I must have overslept, guessing that Drake is playing poker with his brother. Wearing some hip-hugger jeans with a pink v-sweater, some flip flops, and no makeup, I put my blonde hair in a ponytail. I don't want to bother them, so I just stay in the room.

"Sadie, come out here so you can meet Calvin," Drake shouts from the other room.

Walking out to where they're playing poker, I shyly go over to stand beside Drake's chair.

THE STORY OF SADIE FOX

"Cal, this is my wife, Sadie Fox."

*   *   *

CALVIN

I'm chewing on a toothpick and I glance up from watching my cards, unable to believe my eyes. She's freaking gorgeous; that body, her curves, and talk about huge beautiful tits. Her blonde hair is like silk. Flawless skin, her eyes seem like blue diamonds. What do I think? She's sixteen and so young, so innocent looking. My dick twitches, as she shyly says, "Hi," and I can't help it, I want to wrap my muscular arms around her sweet body. I just want to save her, but I realize I can't have those thoughts about her – she's not mine to rescue. I'm thinking, *I never felt like saving anyone before but what has Drake done to her already?* I may seem like a prick, but I'm the brother with the heart. I don't mess with underage girls, I prefer girls my age.

Sadie gives me her hand and says, "Nice to meet you, Calvin," in a sweet, sing-song voice.

As soon as my large hand touches hers, I know, without a doubt, my life will never be the same again. It's like lightning hits me, filling my heart full of electricity.

Trying so badly to contain me, Drake speaks up. "Well, what do you think about my bitch then, Cal?"

"You don't speak like that about your wife, Drake!" I snap back at him. I wanted to beat his ass for bringing her here and for making her his whore. Damn, he's such a dumbass.

"Sadie, I think my brother likes you. Maybe he wants your soft, pink muff too," Drake purrs.

"Shut the fuck up, Drake," I scream back.

"Why? I'll share her with you, bro," he assures me, with a grin on his face.

"What a fucking asshole! I'm out of here."

"Hey, don't be mad, Cal," Drake calls after me and with that, the door slams so hard Sadie jumps up, scared.

*   *   *

DRAKE

"Don't just stand there, Sadie, go to the room. You need some more practice."

She runs to the room and I bring her a six-pack of cheap beer, taking my clothes off as I go. "Well, what are you waiting for, Sadie? Take off those clothes and that damn cotton underwear that I hate you wearing." I open a can of beer. "Here, drink this," I command her.

She's already on the fourth beer and starting to look like she's getting a bit fuzzy on it. Watching her and seeing her relax, I know the beer's doing its job, so I go get one of my sex toys.

"I'm going to play with you first, baby, going to fuck your hooters. I want all my cum all over you." She moans, putting my huge penis between her large tits and I start pumping back and forth. "Yeah, feels good, sweet thing, squeeze your melons tight."

She squeezes tighter, so my cream squirts all over her neck and chest. I was right, she did learn fast. I tie her to the bedpost so I could lick her twat and put a fake phallus up her behind. My licks are rough and her eyes open wide when she sees the sex toy in my hand. "It's just a fake dick that vibrates. Relax, you'll come fast, sweet girl."

Sadie responds very well when I stick my phallus in her love button. She's on top and I stick the vibrator in her anus and she moans. "Get used to it, sweet thing, because two guys will be having intercourse with you soon enough, Sadie, and you'll love it!"

She comes, yelling my name.

"That's right, you will make me lots of money.

THE STORY OF SADIE FOX

All you have to do is drink a six-pack first."

Sadie takes a shower, then changes the bed-sheets, before cleaning my steel pole. She hurries up because she doesn't want to get punished.

Sadie is starting to realize she has feelings for Drake. *How is that even possible? He's a rapist and sex addict who treats me like a slut,* she wonders. Yet she knows he's making her like sex and she understands she's horny for him. *It's like he builds me up and then blows me apart,* she rationalizes to herself.

Waking up with a massive migraine, Drake stirs her to do 'you know what.'

"Sadie, my head hurts," I tell her, grabbing her hair. I add, "Don't ever tell me no, do you hear me, bitch?" She nods her assent. "Now, get on top and ride my thick pole."

Quickly she's on top and I'm biting her huge breasts harder. Sadie, her tits bouncing up and down, I hold her hips, steadying her and putting my finger on her as she closes her eyes. She is so easy to teach. "Going to fuck your behind, sweet girl." I put my condom on and turn her, easing into her apple ass. "Fuck, you're tight, girl."

She yells and I slap her rigid. We both come.

I yank her hair. "Don't yell like that again," I command her, slapping her face. "Go take a shower."

Chapter 4

CALVIN

I'm tattooing Blue Steel on his chest. He's gay and he's been my best friend since we were ten years old. We both own the tattoo shop called Tiger's Den.

"Blue, I'll be gone for a week, babysitting my brother's new bride," I explain.

"Why can't he just take her where he's going, that dumb fuck."

"She's young, Blue, very young, and he's using her as a prostitute, that poor girl. I feel bad for her. He's a fucking rapist."

"Is she that young, Cal?"

"She's sixteen, for Christ's sake. He's training her to be a slut for all the poker guys to have sex with her."

"Wow, sorry, dude. So when he's losing a game, he throws her in the pot? Sorry to say, but your brother is a punk and a monster."

"Your tattoo is coming out great, Blue."

"Thanks, dude. That tiger is just awesome, you're the best. How's your girlfriend doing, Cal?"

"Ah, she's just fine. She's on a trip to China with her boss, at the moment."

"Wow, Cal, you trust Donna with her boss?"

"I don't really care, to be honest."

"Cal, just don't start liking your brother's wife, eh."

"Oh, Blue, she is beautiful. Fuck dude, you'd like her."

"Well then, fuck her – join the poker group."

"Come on, Blue, don't say that. I wouldn't touch a little girl, you know that."

"I know you're an honorable man, Cal. How does she look?"

"Wow, she has diamond-blue eyes, she's fair-complexioned, with huge breasts and a beautiful, curvy body, to die for. I'm not lying; she's a real dream girl, an angel."

"Drake is going to mess her up really bad. He's already fucked her every which way; all the holes filled, I'm guessing."

"Blue, stop! She's a poor, innocent girl."

"I don't know, Cal, you seem to have fallen deeply for this girl."

"Stop saying that."

"I can't, I just want to protect you from your own brother. Come on, Cal, he's a jackass. He always makes the rules and you blindly follow them."

"Whose side are you on, anyway?" I snapped at Blue.

"Yours, obviously, but when it comes to your brother, he is loser number one. You're the good brother. Even if you do look like a bad boy, you have a heart of gold. He will never care about anyone but himself, and that poor girl you say you want to save, well, you're going to get wounded because your brother always loses at all the poker games."

"Let's not talk about this right now. After I finish with your tattoo, we'll go to Dolly's for a beer."

"They never have gay guys there, Cal."

"Hey, we're going for a beer, not to pick up."

"I do like to do both, Cal."

"Blue, you're too much, dude."

"Yeah, that's what all the guys say. With my looks, green eyes, ash-brown short hair, dimples to die for as well as being tall, dark, and handsome, what more can I say?"

We both laugh.

We're at Dolly's. It's a stripper place with girls dancing, stripping, and guys drinking, putting money in the girls' G-strings, swaying like only women could, money hungry; some are beautiful, but not as beautiful as Sadie.

Blue is bored, but there will be a surprise for him as guys come out, swaying also, with G-strings on, their dicks huge. Blue starts to grin now.

"The party is finally starting, Cal," he remarks. "They're gorgeous."

They enjoy the view, with ladies stripping and guys touching their cocks.

"What we have here, Cal, is the best of both worlds. I'm going to be happy tonight. Let's do a foursome?"

"No, Blue, I don't rock like that. I'm going to go home soon to get ready to take care of the princess."

"Okay, mate, just call me if you can't handle her."

I smirk. "I can handle a sixteen-year-old, no problem, but it really saddens me that he's making her into a whore. She's so damn young."

"Yeah, sorry, dude, that your brother is a rapist and a no-good scoundrel and so many more things... oh, and add his gambling problem."

"You know, I truly feel for the girl. He'll break her into tiny little pieces. I can't save her, since she's not mine to save. She's married to him and she'll be trapped in his web of lust, sex, and abuse, dude, like a slave tangled in his perverted world. We can talk trash about Drake all we like, but she's still his."

"All I can say is let them be. He owns her, Cal, so stop trying to be her knight in shining armor. You can't save her, and even if you tried, he's brain-washed her, you're the only one that will get injured."

I look down because I know Blue is right. We went on drinking and enjoying the night, instead. Going into the back room for a lap dance, I decided since I was horny, I'd get myself a fine-looking woman to sit on my dick. Then I'd fuck her, very slow and gentle. I like to treat a woman with respect. I may look like a bad boy, with lots of tattoos, but I like my women to enjoy my package.

I have a seat and she comes in with a smile on her face. She has long, straight, black hair and a beautiful body. They put the music on and she starts swaying to the rhythm, rubbing on my lap with her ass. I hold her waist as my cock enlarges with her every move. Turning toward me, she puts her tits in my face. They're not huge, but very nice all-around. Her pink nipples harden and I suck and lick before I grab her.

"No more dancing, baby. How much for a blowjob?"

"Fifty," she says.

I give her a hundred and remove my jeans along with my boxers. My penis is massive.

"Come on baby, come to daddy," I coo.

She does and, with a smile, she takes the hundred. She starts to blow on my dick. It gives me goosebumps as she sucks real deep, and I eventually cum all over her mouth and down her throat.

Blue had his fun with some guy who was

dancing on stage.

The night is over and we head off home.

Chapter 5

CALVIN

I go to Drake's house. He's left for Vegas already and she's inside, probably looking at cartoons. My sarcasm knows no bounds. I go in with my backpack and could hear the shower running, so I wait on the sofa until she comes out. I scare her.

"Sorry, didn't mean to frighten you, Sadie."

She's holding the white towel tightly in front of her, with drops of water dripping on the floor, all the way to her toes. I bite down on my toothpick – damn, she's a gorgeous young thing. Her face gets so rosy, so I try to stare at the wall and not at her, giving her a smile, to tell her to stop blushing, for God's sake. I know I'm in a dilemma. Blue knew I would fall for this girl who belongs to my brother. *Fuck me! Why me?! I have Donna, but she's always traveling and that's why I have to get blowjobs,* I think. I shake my head sadly.

Sadie gets dressed in her skinny jeans and pink t-shirt; her tits are so huge, it's incredibly hard not to notice. I wish I could devour those breast. *What the hell am I saying? She's just a little girl.*

Taking my thoughts out of the gutter, I ask, "What would you like to do, Sadie?"

"I would like to watch a movie and order some pizza," she softly whispers back.

I smile. "Sure honey, no problem." She smiles at me as if I've just offered her the world. Drake won't give her anything but misery. "Pick the movie, Sadie, while I have the pizza delivered." I know she'll pick a chick-flick since he doesn't have any decent movies of his own.

She comes over with an adorable pout on her lips. "He doesn't have any good movies, just those, horrible, nasty, porno ones. We'll watch regular television then, okay, Calvin?"

"You can call me Cal, if you want," I offer.

She stares at me for a second, then nods her head. "Okay."

We're watching the news. She loves pizza and she's finished half the box already. Where does it go? She has a fine-looking body.

"You want me to bake cookies?" Sadie suggests.

"Sure, honey. We will have to go to the store to buy some stuff. Maybe tomorrow, though." She pouts so adorably. "We'll go in the morning for groceries."

Drake never has any money, so how was she supposed to eat, unless I buy some groceries? That idiot! "It's getting late, Sadie, go to bed now."

She does what I say, really quickly. Watching her sleep, biting on my toothpick, I can't help but notice she's absolutely breathtaking. Sitting on a small sofa in her room, I feel like I have to protect her in some way. I'm drawn to her.

Falling asleep, Sadie wakes me up with some pancakes and bacon and the smell of coffee. She's wearing jean shorts and a white tank-top that shows her huge breasts off.

Will I survive even one day being tempted by that? I have four more days to go. God help me with this girl. My cock is bulging for her, but I would never dare touch her, at her age. *Maybe, when she's eighteen. Knowing Drake, I would probably have to win her at poker. Well, I will wait for that day, because she will be worth the wait. I certainly won't fuck her now. I could show her how to make love properly, so she will never forget me.*

I take Sadie shopping and she was super happy as I bought her some jeans, t-shirts, some sexy lingerie – panties, corsets, crotchless underwear, and some sheer, fishnet bras, all at Drake's request, that stupid ass. I hated doing this, as it is going to take her innocence away, although he already took her virginity, poor girl.

"Calvin!" Turning to her soft voice, she added, "Could we go eat some hamburgers, please?"

"Sure, honey, let's go." I take her to some place called Jake's. It's a small place, a little hole-in-the-wall joint. I'm watching her eat, her luscious lips moving. I just can't help myself. I simply smile at her and she smiles back.

"Calvin, you're not hungry?" she asks.

"Nah, not really."

"Why do you have so many tattoos, if it's okay to ask?"

"Simple – because I like them." Playing with my toothpick with my tongue – I can even do tricks with it – grinning, because my thoughts are so dense. "I am a tattoo artist," I add, in explanation.

"You seem different from your brother."

"I am different, Sadie, very different. Never compare us, please."

"Okay, Calvin, I promise I won't."

She has a pout so cute. I feel for what this girl will suffer at the hands of Drake.

We go home and play checkers before we fall asleep on the sofa, her right next to me. She smells like candy, just like a young girl should smell. I hold her and just watch her beautiful face. It's sad I won't be able to rescue her, but she's not mine to save, I keep reminding myself. I touch her hair and it feels like silk, her skin is so velvety. I'm drawn to her like a bee to honey and I want to kiss her so badly my hands are shaking. Blue was right; I fell for her the moment I saw her. Falling asleep, at some point, we're both holding each other's body for warmth.

CHAPTER 6

CALVIN

The week passed so quickly and now Drake is getting out of the car, along with all his loser friends. I don't want to leave Sadie alone with these assholes. She is in that room, where they will have sex with her, more like rape her; my heart is telling me to stay – and he's bought lots of beer.

"Are you staying, bro, for the poker game?" he asks.

"Yeah, I'm staying. Blue will be here shortly."

"I don't want that fucking gay guy in my

house, bro."

"He's our friend from school, Drake, stop being such an asshole about him. He's my best friend."

"Yeah, your best friend, not mine," Drake snaps back.

"You can be such a prick sometimes. No, make that all the time." He just smirks at me and we all go inside.

We're drinking beer when Drake tells Sadie to parade around these stupid losers. She comes out in a black lace dress. It's so short you could see her butt-cheeks from behind. Her breasts are huge and the guys are in total shock.

One says, "Fuck me, she's stunning. Take the cards out so I can win a fuck with this lovely doll."

Sadie looks scared. He is sweating like a pig, thin, and also missing some front teeth. His hair is all greasy. The heavy guy eating chips and sucking the salt from his fingers has his long hair in a ponytail. He chews on a filthy cigar that looks like he'd had it in his mouth forever. Damn sick guys. Another one is smoking, one after another, and has an awful case of acne. Whoever wins will be touching her. My heart is bleeding for my lovely Sadie.

Blue barges in, slamming the door loudly and getting everyone's attention.

"Hey, dude," he greets me. We slap hands. He turns to Drake and smirks at him. "Nice seeing you again, Drake and friends. Let's play."

Blue whispers to me, "God, Cal, these guys are utterly repulsive."

He made me laugh. Poor Sadie, that wretched girl is going to vomit.

We're all sitting and Drake is shuffling the cards. He yells for Sadie to bring beers for all the guys.

Blue watches her. He leans in and whispers to me again. "She's an absolute beauty, Cal, no wonder you like her."

"No kissing over there, you two gay boys,"

Drake taunts us.

"Shut the fuck up, Drake," I snarl.

We all have our cards and each hand is worth twenty dollars. We're drinking our beers.

"Sadie, go drink your six-pack of beer, go to the room," Drake commands her.

She leaves and nobody could take his eyes off her ass as she walked away. Dan, the acne-riddled guy, puts his sunglasses on. The greasy guy, Ray, just stares at his cards. He always has a face like he's bluffing. Biting on my toothpick, I look at Blue with a mischievous grin.

"Cal, you'd better win, or she'll get fucked by one of these ugly morons," he mouths to me. Everyone shows their cards and I win, with seven, eight, nine, ten, and a jack. We play half the night. Blue and I lose, with the heavy, greasy guy, Ruben, winning. My heart aches for Sadie.

Ruben can't wait to go with Sadie. Drake tells him to go to the room on the right and not to be shy. I stare directly at Drake – how could he do this to his young wife?

Blue tells me to let it go. "Cal, you don't want to be here and wait for this dude to finish."

We go outside for a smoke. I didn't want to leave her with that loser. I didn't even finish my cigarette when I heard her screams. I turn. Blue grabs my arm to stop me from going anywhere. My heart is filled with pain and all I do is put my head down.

*   *   *

SADIE

This guy is so gross. He slapped me on my ass so roughly, he bit my nipples, and he made me suck his dirty cock. When he pulled my hair, I started to vomit and he hit me, telling me to clean up the mess. He said he wasn't going to leave until he got his money's worth. I cleaned the mess and then he kissed me.

"Take your clothes off and drink some beer, girl."

I do as he says. His smell made me want to vomit all over again.

"Lie on the bed and open your legs, sweetie," he commands me. He plays with my tits. "Wow! Sweetie! You have huge jugs."

He sucks them, then he licks my muff. It's hard not to come as he pinches my nipples while he sucks, sweating like a pig. The smell was unbearable as he's rubbing his hard penis on my sweet spot and pushes it inside me. I yell, but he has no mercy on me. He's just banging me, yeah!

"Sweetie, you slut, fuck me, come on sweet thing," he murmurs. He pulls out and comes all over my body. My tears flow and I feel filthy, dirty. His odor was dreadful and I just want to heave so bad. "Thanks, sweet thing, you're a good fuck. Now, drink your beer."

He walks out of the room and I take a shower,

hating myself. I'm a dirty girl now, a whore. Falling on the tile floor, I ask myself, *Why I am doing this?*

*   *   *

Calvin scares me. He's standing by my bed asking me, "Are you okay, Sadie?" My tears drip down my cheeks, my lips are trembling and he opens his arms to hold me.

"Anytime you want to leave Drake, just let me know. He will use and abuse you. This is wrong, Sadie. I can't help you if you want to stay with him."

"Get off our bed and out of our room, Calvin. I'm going to have sex with my wife," Drake interrupts.

Cal leaves me with Drake, slamming the door as he departs. Drake sucks my boobs while he puts his finger in my mouth, gasping that he loves licking my nipples. I am starting to love this man, he turns me on with porn and he gives me beer. I had two beers left from the six-pack.

He turns me around and pushes his junk way inside. We have a pleasurable, sexually intense climax. I know, deep down, Drake is using me, but he was making me want him more, every day. As time passes, having sex, teaching me to want and need sex, I started to require it, almost like a drug. He gave me something to make me so horny that I needed an orgasm five times a day. When he wasn't around, I would pleasure myself; it was such a satisfaction.

I'm taking a shower alone, washing my hair, and water is splashing over my tits, getting me sizzling hot. Putting soap on my hand, I massage my breasts, moaning. I squeeze my areolas. Hmmmm! It feels superior when my fingers slide, with my soapy hands, into the inner walls of my love button. This won't take long, pleasuring myself. My sounds are piercing, I'm biting my bottom lip, my orgasm is so passionate. I wash all the soap away and dry my tingling body before getting dressed.

I start to clean the house from the poker game. The guys made a mess and it really smells bad. I make myself something to eat and am watching television when Drake tells me to go to the red room. That's what he calls it. I'm guessing he must have lost in a poker game, again.

"Go with a sheer black tank and a G-string," he tells me.

How did I end up like this? Going from a re-spectable young girl to a slut? Going with the wrong guy on a date, that's how. This guy walks in and tells me he just wants me to suck his prick. He looks decent enough and he just stands there as I lick it first, then suck it continuously without gag-ging, because Drake will hit me if I do. I'm always scared that I'll make a mistake. I don't want any-one to hurt me, so I strive to obey and every day that passes it gets harder to be a sex-slave. Calvin is a kind guy, though. He always comes over to see how I am. He's very sweet and it's funny that they're brothers because they really are like darkness and daylight.

*   *   *

Months pass. I've been drinking a six-pack five days a week. Drake told me I had to drink it so I would relax and have sex with the guys he brought home. My sex drive is in overdrive – always on the top of my list: needing sex. With those guys it didn't matter if they were short, stunk, or the good, the bad, and the ugly, I was getting my fix. Drake made me do things that would shame any mother. I obeyed him, of course – he was my husband and the master of my universe, so to speak. How did I get down this road of destruction that would be the death of me? I was ashamed, every morning, when I stared at myself in the mirror, feeling disgusted with myself.

When my birthday came around, Drake gave

me four guys to have sexual intercourse with, as a gift. He gave me a pill to loosen up, though. I think it was to unwind me, but it made me so aroused I had to drink a six-pack. All those guys spanked and had sex with me roughly. I was tied up while Drake was playing poker with the rest of the guys, and I had a full-length penis in every single hole.

My life was appalling and I wanted to run away, escape, hide under a rock, but he made me needy for sex and for this lifestyle. I haven't seen Calvin for a while. He's staying away, who can blame him? He did have a girlfriend who came home from her travels from time to time. He's started to be my best friend, as he cares what happens to me. We eat pizza together and he likes to get wet, outside, in the rain. He's a young kid at heart and he is younger than Drake.

My hair is in a ponytail. I'm watering the front yard, getting horny again, and the neighbor, who is fixing his car, keeps watching me. I can't fuck that guy, or actually, I could. With my finger, calling him over, he runs to me. We go to the red room and he smells of dirty sweat. What the hell! I'm too horny to care, so we do the bad deed. He knew all the right buttons to push – what great sex! Fuck! My shame for this game knows no end. It's eating me up.

Dottie comes by, once in a while, to visit. She doesn't look that good, these days; her boyfriend gave her drugs and she's completely hooked now.

*   *   *

CALVIN

My mind is totally haywire just thinking about Sadie having sex act with all those guys. It's driving me crazy. I'm starting to hate Drake with a vengeance. My heart wants her so badly. I won't touch her until she's eighteen, but until then I'll be keeping an eye on her. I'm so messed up by loving that girl, but your heart chooses whom to love. Blue is keeping at me about her. It's ironic when you think about it. He worries so much about me and he has been my friend for so long; we connect on so many levels.

Chapter 7

CALVIN

It's Sadie's eighteenth birthday and Drake was having a huge poker game where the winner of that game will get her for the night. She's going to be mine all night. I've waited three years for this. My girlfriend left me because I didn't want to marry her. As soon as I laid eyes on Sadie, it was love at first sight. Sadie has changed, though, she's not that innocent sixteen-year-old girl anymore. Drake's used her and abused her in the world of sex, lust, and even some BDSM. They've tied her up, spanked her, and whipped her.

THE STORY OF SADIE FOX

For the first time, my tears rolled down my face as she was yelling and crying, saying no. I couldn't save her and my heart aches for her. For all of these three years, I have been her friend, doing normal things with her, like watching movies, eating junk food, and playing with water balloons outside; she was such a carefree, beautiful girl. Tonight she will be mine.

Blue is playing also, just in case I don't win. He will make sure no one else will touch her tonight. I yearn for her and I want to show her what making love is truly like. She will discover the difference between having sex for a six-pack and making love. At this point, I want to murder Drake for what he has done to this poor girl. She is mine and she always will be. All those three years, I have tried to make her life tolerable. She always wanted Drake, though, like he'd brainwashed her. Giving her a six-pack of beer is horrible, just so she could tolerate those losers. Drake brings them home five days a week. Sadie was always in that red room waiting for whatever worthless bastard would win the prize – and believe me, she is a prize.

She's standing, smiling at me. What a beautiful sight she is. Her long blonde hair like silk. She's wearing sexy, sheer lingerie, and I grin back.

"Let's get the party started," Blue says, walking toward me.

Drake and his buddies smirk.

"Are we all sitting?" Blue asks, with a smile on his face.

At the poker table, there are four of Drake's loser friends, as well as Blue and I, drinking some mixed drinks. Drake yells at Sadie to drink her first beer from the six-pack. I beam at him and Sadie stares at me. I nod at her not to drink that beer, she nods back but she answers him, "Okay Drake."

Blue shuffles the cards; I'm biting my toothpick and my sweat is starting to drip down the side of my face. I have to win her, or my heart will break into so many fragments. We all put one hundred dollars on the table and we get three cards. Everyone's face is focused on the cards. Jim is sweating like a hog; Jerry, the thin guy with greasy hair, looks like he hasn't bathed for weeks; and Grey is just a kid. He's twenty-one, but he looks like a fifteen-year-old – mind you, he plays poker very well. Everyone holds their cards and Blue smiles. I stare at my cards and the guys grin. I know they're bluffing and we go another round of betting. We receive our final cards and we all show our cards. Jim wins with three aces, the jerk, and says he can't wait to tap that young thing. I wanted to beat his ass. These jerks are making me want to kill them if they keep talking about her that way. We play another game; I don't know how many toothpicks I broke – my nerves are hitting me like a bolt of lightning.

"Hey, Cal, you're sweating profusely," Blue mutters to me, quietly.

"If I lose, Blue, one of these jerks will have sex

with her," I strangle back to him.

"Cal, she's been screwing all these dudes, sorry to say, for years. So, what is it about today that's special, dude?"

"It's her eighteenth birthday, Blue! I waited for her, I couldn't touch her until she was of age, you know this."

"Yeah, Cal, I get it, but there's so many fish in the sea, why her? Why put yourself through such misery, anyway? No matter what happens tonight, she's still your brother's wife."

Drake clears his throat. "Are you two playing?" he sneers. "Or are you going to chatter like girlfriends? Shut the hell up!"

Blue gets upset. "Let's play, then," he grumbles. "And if I win, I'm going to kick Drake's ass, big-time."

Drake laughs so loudly he chokes on his cognac and spills some on his black suit. He's only drinking cognac because one of the guys brought it. He is so cheap, he always buys Milwaukee Best, a damn lousy beer that leaves a bad taste in your mouth. I always bring my own beer, which is Heineken.

We play all night and in the last game we put all our money down. Drake says, "Let's make this interesting. Let's play for a thousand dollars, winner takes all."

We all have our cards and every guy is desperate to win since the prize is so high. Blue and I are staring at the losers, all sweating, drinking, laughing, along with some nervous talking. So, we're sitting here, ready to play another game, another hand of poker. I'm flicking my toothpick rhythmically. This dirty, filthy, smelly piglet, all anxious. Little does he realize, I don't even have a good hand. With over a thousand dollars on the table, I go all in.

Blue just stares at me, in shock, like always. Drake folds, along with two other guys. They're like dogs, tails between their legs, even though he had three-of-a-kind and I didn't have anything.

"I lost, Blue," I lament softly.

Drake just laughs.

That grease-ball won her. My heart is aching for what he will do to her. Drake yells, "Your best friend didn't win, sorry, dear, he never could play poker good, hahaha!"

"Shut that mouth up, asshole," I scream at him.

The jerk that won runs into the red room, where Sadie was. She doesn't yell or make noise and I'm guessing that's a good sign.

I leave with Blue and we go to some bar, where we drink until daylight.

After going home and sleeping all day, my phone starts ringing and ringing.

"Hello!"

"It's Blue, Cal. You better go to the hospital."

"Why? What's up?"

"Sadie is in the hospital."

He doesn't go into details, so I get dressed, get

on my motorcycle, and tear off. My jaw is ticking like a time bomb. If that motherfucker's hurt her, I'm going to fuck him up so badly and kill that fucker.

I park the bike, take off my helmet, and stare at the front of the hospital, biting on my toothpick. I know it's going to be bad. When I step into her room, Blue is sitting at the end of her bed and she is asleep. She's was beaten up so badly, plus they gave her a ton of drugs and then five guys banged her. Blue was telling me everything and my tears burst, like a flowing dam, spilling down my face. I walk toward her, holding her soft hand as I take a seat. Of course, my sleaze ball brother wasn't around so I could beat the crap out of him.

Sadie squeezes my hand as she wakes up, with tears cascading down her face. It breaks my heart and I want to leave because I didn't like feeling so guilty about what happened. Leaving this girl is going to kill me, one day, of a broken heart.

"How are you feeling, love?" I ask softly.

She tries to smile, but it hurts for her to move. I kiss her forehead and I stay with her for three days. I'm taking her home because Drake went off to Vegas. He truly doesn't care about Sadie. I tell Blue I'll be taking a week off from our tattoo shop to take care of her. He never questions me, as he knows me so well, sometimes more than I do myself. I head for home to clean the house and fix up a room for her. I'd do anything for that girl, after all she has gone through. I wanted to scream, "Why God?! Why her, such an innocent girl?" I just can't walk away from her.

I love Sadie Fox with all my heart. Why does love hurt this way? After howling by myself in pity, I determine that one day she will be mine, completely. I never, ever thought love could break you into pieces and strip your heart and soul like this does to me.

* * *

THE STORY OF SADIE FOX

Laying her gently on the bed. She was sleeping softly as I watched her beautiful silhouette. My heart was beating faster than a speeding car and my hands trace her features. She has gone through so much, my heart breaks for her. On my stomach, I have a tattoo of her in her wet t-shirt, nipples hardened, showing her blonde hair cascading down her shoulders and showing off her lovely long legs, with jean shorts. It was the best tattoo on my entire body.

Making some lunch, some hot soup and some sandwiches, I take it to her. She's awake as I take the tray, with orange juice and a People magazine. She smiles her thank you.

"Calvin, that's very sweet of you to stay with me. I promise to get better so I won't be a burden to you." She starts to choke on the soup.

"Slow down, sweetheart," I instruct her and begin to feed her the rest. "Okay, what movie do you want to watch. I have three to choose from: *Broke-Back Mountain, Pretty in Pink,* or *The Break-*

fast Club?"

Of course she chose *Pretty in Pink.* Blue always makes me watch that damn movie but I won't complain because this is not about me, it's all about Sadie and I would move heaven and earth hoping that she sees how much I love her. We also play some checkers, until she falls into a peaceful sleep.

Chapter 8

CALVIN

S adie is sitting on my porch with her arms around her legs, deep in thought. My heart wants her but will she ever want me? She's too good for me. Blue keeps telling me she's a slut, that Drake made her filthy. We fought about it and I told him never to talk about her like that. She's mine and I've felt only tenderness and love since the moment my eyes met her diamond-blue eyes and they took me to a place where I wanted to be – submerged in her soul. I wanted to swim in those deep blue ocean eyes of Sadie Fox. Holding my breath that one day she could love me too, someday, in this lifetime.

"Calvin, let's take a walk!" she suggests.

"Of course, baby-doll, anything your heart desires." Her smile could make my heart float and totally rock my boat. Holding her hand was heaven. I'm not the type of guy who does this sort of gesture, but for Sadie, I would go to dreamland to give her paradise. "How are you feeling, baby girl?" I ask softly.

"I'm okay, Calvin. Don't worry about me; strong is my middle name." We both laugh. She is tough, but for how long, I keep asking myself. We buy some pizza, drink sodas, and watch *The Fast and the Furious*. She comes closer to me and my penis does a couple of twitches. Telling myself not to get too close to this baby because I know I won't be able to stop myself from touching that lustful, beautiful body, I squirm away. I'm in agony as she makes herself more comfortable. I couldn't take it any longer. God forgive me, I carry her to my bed. Staring straight into her ocean eyes, I whisper, "Let me make love to you, Sadie. Let me be the one to treat you the way you deserve."

"What about Drake," she protests.

"The hell with him, he doesn't care about you," I exclaim forcefully. "Sadie, please just give me this night." She nods agreement. Wetting my lips, I begin kissing her all over, so gently. I touch her hair and loosen her ponytail, allowing her beautiful, silky, blonde hair to cascade onto the pillow, kissing every inch of her face. I don't want to miss any part of her flesh. All I hear is the whimpering sound she is making and I feel my dick grow, inch by inch. Kissing her arms, I slaver each finger, very slowly.

"Cal!" she calls out my name.

"What, baby? I'm going to rock your world."

Continuing this beautiful torture, my pain – her pleasure – not missing an inch of Sadie's skin, I couldn't help growling like a wolf in heat. Her whimpers are driving me senseless – licking her breasts, sucking on one teat, then the other.

"Cal, that feels good," she murmurs.

"Yes, baby, I'm going to make you cum very soon." I'm lavishing kisses on her stomach until I reach my ultimate destination. Taking a deep breath and smelling her scent was utterly divine. Opening her pussy lips, I whisper, "Don't move, baby," before blowing on her muff. "Baby, let me pleasure you, my sweetness." I'm using my finger and tongue to play with her inner walls. Teasing and pleasing her is my goal in life now. She was pulling my hair for further satisfaction. I was willing to give my heart and soul to the only one woman I'd ever loved. She was thrashing around, with my tongue lashing, and with so much love, she came all over my mouth. Hmm! It was like tasting wine and strawberries; the combination was astonishing. I was not finished with her yet, though, kissing her on her forehead.

"Calvin?"

THE STORY OF SADIE FOX

"Yes, Sadie."

"Why do you care about me so much?"

Staring straight into her diamond-blue eyes, my own eyes tear up. "Because I love you, Sadie, it's that simple. Since the very first day, I couldn't stop it. My love for you just filled my heart and there was no getting around it."

"You can't love me, Calvin, I belong to Drake!" she protests.

"Let's not talk about Drake. He doesn't love you, Sadie."

"But he's still my husband," she argues.

"I'll help you leave him. We could have babies, we could get married, and I could make you so happy, Sadie. Just think about it, please. Leave him or he will destroy you. Promise me."

"Okay, Cal, but I do love him."

"How could you love a man that uses you and abuses you every which way?" Tears burst forth from me, like water from a dam. Holding her, I whisper, "Sorry, baby, I didn't mean to hurt you!"

"You've never hurt me, Calvin, not intention- ally, anyway," she reassures me.

"I wouldn't," I swear.

Turning to make love with her, I relax, giving her kisses all over her body. I can't help it, I'm so turned on by her and my tongue-ring did wonders to her muff and soft skin, rocking her world. Kiss- ing her huge breasts, I didn't want this love-mak- ing to end but everything special comes to an end; that's just the reality of life.

We make love all night and even if she couldn't love me, she'll always remember this night. Making love with Sadie Fox is a dream come true. I would never love anyone else again. She's now in my veins, my heart, and my soul.

*   *   *

Drake called to tell me to take Sadie back to the house. I was taking a shower, with the hot water streaming over my face and my cries wracking my soul. I didn't want her with him; my heart was going to be shattered but this was out of my control. "God, please! Don't let him hurt her anymore," I railed. Wiping my tears away with a towel, I get on my motorcycle and wait for her. She bounds up to me with her short-shorts on. My eyes get watery. I put my toothpick in my mouth, so I won't say, "Don't go back. I love you so much, please stay with me. Be with me, love me. I could make you happy." Swallowing my words so they wouldn't upset her, we put our helmets on and we're on our way. I had to go to work and let Blue go home for some rest. He has been beyond a friend, he's a brother to me.

*　　*　　*

BLUE STEEL

"I'm worried about Cal," I tell Ken.

"He's a big boy, Blue! He can look after himself."

"You don't know him like I do."

"Hmmm, am I supposed to be jealous of him?" Ken responds.

"No, honey, I don't cheat when I'm in a relationship. I'm very committed."

Ken Watson is my boyfriend and my lover. He is gay and we've been together for a few months. It's so tough to find a perfect gay guy who could love you and not cheat on you. I'm starting to love him and he means a lot to me. "Calvin loves Sadie Fox but I don't think it's mutual. For some crazy reason, she loves that creep of a husband of hers. Cal's brother is a low-life. One day he'll get his; someone will kill him. The way he gambles, always losing, giving Sadie to those jerks who abuse her so terribly, using sex toys on her."

"Just stay out of it, Blue," Ken warns me. "He will get tired of pursuing her for no result and find someone else to love and have children with.

You'll see, Blue. He's a smart man. There's only so much a man can take. If he can't save her, he'll leave. Hey, there's lots of fish in the sea, right?"

We change the subject; we didn't see eye to eye about this situation, so we leave it alone.

CHAPTER 9

DRAKE

I'm super-pissed now! Sadie has become very ill. She can't eat and it's been two months since she last saw Calvin. She keeps asking for him as she's lying on the bed, vomiting. I give up and call for a doctor.

Sadie starts to cry, so I slap her and tell her to shut the hell up. I'm bloody nervous, as I need the bitch to help pay my debts. The doctor informs me that she's two months pregnant. In utter disbelief, I thank and pay him.

Running into Sadie, I shout, "It's his, isn't it?

Answer me, you whore."

She starts weeping. "I don't know, Drake!"

"Well, it's fucking not mine, Sadie. I used a condom." I grab her arms, shaking her. "You bitch, fucking my brother, you goddamn whore." I'm fuming to hell, as she just stands there blubbering something. "Come here," I yell.

I hit her and she falls back on the bed, where I start striking her stomach with my fists, over and over, my vicious anger drowning my brain. I didn't even hear her screams. When I finally stopped, her body had gone limp and blood was all over the comforter. Feeling her pulse, I decide she'll live. "Damn bitch!" I scream in frustration.

Calling the doctor to check on her, he confirmed she'd lost the baby and gave her some meds to allow her to sleep.

Days passed and she couldn't move at all, so I had to call off the poker games, because she was out of commission, for now, at least. I needed a break from them anyway, as I'd been losing quite a bit, lately.

I told the doctor to give her some birth control, so he put in an IUD.

When she eventually woke up, with tears of sorrow in her eyes, she asked about her baby.

"What happened? The baby's dead? NO! NO! Please, no! That was our baby!"

"Shut the hell up, Sadie. It wasn't ours, it was yours and Calvin's. So just shut the fuck up!"

*   *   *

SADIE

I shed tears of pain and grief and fell into a deep depression. I now had no life inside me, but I was no longer scared if he would beat me again. What he did, I'll never forget that. He murdered my baby. With my body so weak, Drake kept insisting

THE STORY OF SADIE FOX

I needed to eat.

"You'd better eat, you bitch," he was always shouting at me.

Closing my eyes, I wished I was dead. This isn't a life! Where is Calvin? I want to see him, want him to hold me, with the strength and love he has for me. With sleepy eyes I fell into a deep and unfathomable sleep, my heart shattered, and my life had no significance anymore. I dreamt of my baby boy, running, calling for his mommy and me opening my arms to him. He looked exactly like Calvin, with his light brown hair bouncing, his hazel eyes, and his fair skin. He was absolutely adorable. My heart hurts because I didn't want to wake up. When I did, I noticed my pillow was soaked with tears of loss. Utter loneliness swept over me, missing my friend Calvin. I don't know what to do about my life as a slut. Maybe it was for the best to lose the baby. What mother would raise a child in this kind of life? I finally convince myself that it was best for all of us.

* * *

CALVIN

I put all my attention and effort into my business at Tiger's Den. With a toothpick in my mouth, I'm deep in thought. I haven't seen Sadie for a couple of months and my heart is begging for her. My penis is wanting her even more, but I've got to put my mind into my job, first. It's a lost cause, I know it. Sadie doesn't want to leave Drake, so he'll take advantage of her. I can't rescue the love of my life.

"Cal, where are you?" I hear. I'm tattooing a customer at the time.

"Right here, Blue," I shout. "What is it?"

"I hate giving you bad news, but I was playing poker with some guys who know your brother. They said he was bragging that he beat Sadie so bad she lost her baby, because it wasn't his and he couldn't afford to have her pregnant. He didn't even take her to the hospital, dude, he just called the doctor to check on her."

"What a son-of-a-bitch!" I screamed in horror. "I'm going to kill that mother-fucker."

I finish the client's tattoo, grabbing my leather jacket on the way out, and sit on my motorcycle, my jaw shaking with fury. All I wanted to do was strangle him to death.

"Where is Sadie?" I scream at him, as I slam into the house.

Drake rolls his eyes. "Get the fuck out of my house, Cal. You have no business here."

"Where is she, you bastard?"

"She's in her room. She got sick," he finally told me.

I go and grab Drake around the neck, squeezing with all my might. How I wanted to take his last breath with my bare hands – they were trembling. I let go of this pathetic animal, this so fucking sadistic poor excuse for a man, throwing him against the wall, then the floor, and kicking him in his ribs for good measure. Fucking snake! I never thought I could hate my brother so much, but he is a monster.

I go looking for my love. She's crying on the bed.

"Calvin," she whimpers.

I hold her tightly. "Baby, what happened?"

"I got pregnant, it was our baby, Calvin. Drake found out and he killed our baby. He beat me, hit my stomach, my arms, all over," she pitifully cried.

I held her securely, tears dropping from my eyes.

"It was my baby, Calvin. I dream of him all the time. It was going to be a boy and he looked just like you." I held her, the whole night, while she was sobbing for our lost baby.

It's morning and I ask her to come and live with me.

"I can't," she sobs in my arms.

I left her with that beast of a brother, giving

her a sweet kiss before I go. I head back to work, no shower, just shattered and heavy-hearted. I didn't talk to anyone that week. I went to a bar, got drunk and slept around, trying to numb the pain, but it was all in vain. Taking a woman from the bar to my house, we walk in, drinking until I drop, but this girl had other plans, taking my clothes off. We were nude and I was pretending it was Sadie. She starts to feel my tool, which was ready to shoot in her mouth. She drank my cream like a winner. But I knew it didn't matter whom I'm with if it's not Sadie Fox, the love of my life, my heart, and soul, the one I would die for, at any time, any day, any place, it just doesn't work.

I go to the 7-Eleven to buy two coffees so she could go home. When I return to my house, she's under my sheets and she peeks out at me. Her hair is brunette and it's wild, messy-looking, beautiful, with her green, oval eyes staring at me. I fancy her – she's pretty.

"I bought some coffee."

"Thanks." She smiles. She drinks very carefully, so as not to burn her lips. "Cal, that's just what I need." Her smile is pleasant.

"I'm going to work now, so take your time, okay?"

"Cal, do you want to go for a date?"

"Sure, there's a movie I want to see. How about next week? Put down your number on the paper over there."

"Sure thing, baby," she responds gleefully.

I had to depart, as I had some clients to tattoo. They wanted portraits on their backsides and it would take me all day.

*   *   *

CALVIN

My day was going quickly – hearing the machine buzz was my distraction from Sadie. She's so damaged, she feels she has to live that kind of life. I can't live this way anymore so I've got to let her go, starting with dating other women. She's never been mine to salvage. Blue comes in with his boyfriend.

"Hey, Cal, what's up?" he asks.

"Not much, dude."

"We're going to a club, it's called Smooth Glitter. Want to go, Cal?"

"Sure, mate. I'm going to invite a girl I met last night, if that's cool?"

"Okay, it's a plan," Blue answers.

Closing my shop and heading home, I notice the woman had left her name and number next to the kitchen table. I called Gracie Clarkson.

"Hello! Hey, how about going to a club, Gracie?" I ask.

"I would love to go, Cal."

"Tonight?"

She gives me her address and I'm on my way, driving my black mustang. Gracie looks fantastic

– a short, sexy red dress, red heels, with her dark, sexy hair flowing with the wind, luxurious glossy purple lips, swaying her hips, and with a lovely smile on her face. All I can think of, though, is not having Sadie in my life and that ache in my heart, that hole that no one else can fill. But, I'm willing to try anything to forget her and my recurring thoughts of her kissing those smelly assholes. I'm going insane not knowing if they're hurting Sadie, but she's not mine to rescue, so I've got to go on with my life and maybe have a couple of kids. I want to wake up with a warm body in my arms. Something is always snagging me, in my heart, to save Sadie.

Gracie kisses me, taking me away from my thoughts of Sadie, the love of my life. Gracie, purple lipstick tasting like grape, has made my penis rock-hard.

We meet Blue at Smooth Glitter, a club that everyone is going to in this town. When something new comes along, it will be a hit for all the bored people and the younger crowd that are sick of small bars. We start to dance and I realize I haven't had as good a time as this for a long time. For once, my thoughts were with someone else.

*   *   *

SADIE

I wasn't the same after losing my baby. When Drake lost at poker, I would be like a zombie, drinking my six-pack of beers to be numb and let those dirty old men touch and fuck me. I miss my best friend, Cal. It's been a couple of months since he told me to go with him and I said no. He hasn't come to our house, not even to play poker. Who could hold him accountable for me? I hurt him all the time, so maybe he found someone new and hates me now for letting him down. I hate myself. How can I ever love him when in a sadistic, twisted way, I love Drake? He cheats on me, he sells me to the highest bidder, he's a loser in a suit with a black heart, a handsome devil in a suit with a sex drive. It's true what they say – 'women yearn for the bad boys.' Drake fools people with his disguise as a cool guy, but his heart is black lava. I love the man that messed me up for the rest of my life, the killer that killed my baby boy. Life has no meaning, alone, in my own world of destruction. I'm lost and my heart aches – depression kicking in and having no joy.

Dottie got into drugs, so she doesn't come around anymore. I don't have any friends; I have no hope, only the despair of loneliness. With tears slipping down my pillow, I think of Cal. "Come to me, Cal. I miss you, my friend," I whisper softly as I'm falling asleep. Cal never comes, though, only in my dreams, along with our baby boy.

Chapter 10

DRAKE

I have lots of poker games coming up, so Sadie better be in tip-top shape. She's my bread and butter, she's an absolute champion. I have to make sure she doesn't get pregnant, though. She wants babies, but that bitch will not have kids if I have anything to do with it, and if she ever does, she will give them away. I need her! All the guys want her, she is beautiful. With that body and a low-priced six-pack of beer, she gives the guys what they want. I did well making her my whore.

I hear vomiting. What the hell! Sadie is on her

knees next to the toilet.

"What the hell is wrong with you now, Sadie?"

"I feel ill," she mutters.

"You'd better not be with child, because I will beat you up good if you are."

She gets sicker, though, and I pull her hair and throw her on the bed.

The doctor's checking her and I'm walking back and forth. My biggest nightmare is she's having a baby. Who knows who the baby's father is. I don't have sex with her, and she's been screwing all my friends on the poker team. I talk to the doctor, asking him to give me something so she could lose the baby.

He stares at me like I'm some sort of monster. "Why won't you let her have this baby, Drake? Let that poor girl have her nine months and let her be in peace."

"Because she makes money for me, Doc. Please don't make me beat her up."

*   *   *

CALVIN

I call the police and take Sadie home with me, so she can have this baby. I know I can't keep her long, but at least until she's a few more months along, so that bastard can't kill this baby. That poor girl has gone through so much and she deserves my help.

The cops take Drake to jail and allow me to take Sadie to my house. My wife takes care of her while I'm at work.

*   *   *

DRAKE

A few months later, I pick her up at Cal's house. She's showing, so she is no use to me, so I'll be touring poker games in different states. I told Cal to take care of Sadie. He didn't want to, but he can't say no when it's the love of his life. He does have a wife now, she moved in last week. I can't wait to see how this story plays out, as no woman likes being second. Sadie is asleep, so I leave her a note:

Dear Sadie,

I will be gone until you have that baby, so don't get too comfortable, my sweetie. You owe lots of money and your payback will be a bitch. Calvin will come over to see how you're doing. Don't miss me too much, because while you are getting fat, I'll be fucking lots of beautiful women that are thin.

Your lover boy, Drake

*   *   *

CALVIN

"Hi, Sadie, how are you?" I greet her.

"Calvin, I've missed you," she exclaims. We hug and she smells so good, giving me a kiss on my cheek. She looks healthy, also.

"So, is everything all right? Have you gone to the doctor?"

"I'm going today, going to get my first ultrasound. Cal, could you take me, please?"

"Of course, Sadie, you're my best girl."

We're at the doctor's office and she's lying on the bed. The doctor greets us and puts some gel on Sadie's stomach. The heartbeat is fast.

"Done," the doctor declares. "You want to know what you're having?"

"Yes!" Sadie squeals, excitedly.

We could see the little figure of a ball. "It's a girl, Sadie," the doc pronounces.

"A girl, OMG!" she screams. I held her hand

and my heart was aching for her. Wanting her was my weakness. "Cal, all of a sudden I'm craving a huge cheeseburger with chilli fries."

It was tough not to laugh; she's so happy and going to be a good mother – that is if my brother lets her have this baby.

We're eating and I just had to ask, "Who's the father, Sadie?"

"I don't know. It's certainly not Drake's. He doesn't have sex with me anymore."

That fucking prick, I'm thinking to myself. He's just passing her around to his filthy, nasty friends when he loses at poker.

After we finish eating, I take her home, where we make popcorn and watch a movie. She falls asleep leaning on my shoulder, and all I could do is wish that she was mine, and this was my baby. Carrying her to the bed, I leave to go home to Gracie. Gracie's just told me she was having my baby and I'm supposed to be happy about that, but I'm not.

It's not fair for her either, but trying to go on with my life, without Sadie Fox, it's a struggle. She's my drug of choice and I could literally see her waste away.

"So, why did you come home so late, Calvin?"

"I had to help out a friend," I answer.

"What's his name?"

"It's not a guy. She is my brother's wife, Sadie. She's pregnant and all alone."

"All you have to do is tell me, Cal, so I won't worry about you," she assures me.

"Sorry, babe. I'm going tomorrow to take her to buy some groceries."

"Are you going to be her slave every day?" she asks, sarcasm dripping off her lips.

"Don't say it like that, honey. I'm just a kind guy trying to do a good deed, that's all."

"Well... let me show you how good I could be, Cal." She grins.

We start to kiss, our tongues dancing in the moonlight. I remove her dress. She has my baby safe in her tummy. I get on my knees, kissing every inch of her tummy and body, showing her some love. After all, she is the mother of my child.

*   *   *

SADIE

I was so happy to see Cal, but he seems so distant with me now. He always has been an honorable kind of guy. I know he has boundaries and a life besides me, though.

A few months pass and my tummy is huge. I'm wobbling all over the house and my back has been aching. Cal hasn't come since my last doctor's appointment and that was a month ago. I'm seven months now and lying on the bed with pain, but I don't want to bother anyone.

"Ouch!" I shout. One hour later, my pain is worse and tears are dripping down my cheeks.

I'm squirming with discomfort, squeezing the sheets for dear life, when I hear a door slam. It's Blue.

"Hey, sweetheart, what's wrong?" he inquires.

"I'm in labor and I'm scared. I'm only seven months."

Blue takes out his cell phone. "Cal, you'd better get over here. It's Sadie and she's in labor."

Calvin comes. It seemed like hours, but he actually came fifteen minutes later.

"Cal, it hurts," I whimper.

"I know, baby girl."

I yell so loudly.

"Open your legs, Sadie. Fuck! The baby's head is showing. OMG! Blue, bring some towels and hot water, quickly."

"Sure thing," he replies. He runs out.

"Don't push yet, baby girl," Cal warns.

"Cal, I'm scared."

"Hang in there, baby," he offers.

*   *   *

CALVIN

She yells in anguish and I tell her to push. She's in so much pain but the baby is coming. "One more push, baby, one more push," I tell her.

All of a sudden, the baby starts to scream and we all smile, but then she goes totally silent.

"OMG! Cal, why is she not crying anymore?" Sadie wails.

The paramedics arrive and take them both to the hospital. With the baby only four pounds, she's placed in an incubator. Sadie is resting, they gave her meds so she could sleep, so I called Drake. The prick was having sex and a girl said he would be there soon, probably to do something to the baby or to Sadie.

I call Gracie and tell her that I'm staying with Sadie until Drake comes home. She wasn't happy, but I could not fault her.

"You are always saving her, Cal. When will it stop? You love her, not me. I'm the one having your baby, not her. She's just your brother's slut."

"Shut the hell up, Gracie. Stop talking about her like that. You don't even know her, or what my brother did to her."

"That's none of your business," she bites back. "She's not your wife, so stay away from her."

"Come on, stop being so jealous, Gracie. It's not good for you to get upset over nothing."

"Calvin, just leave her alone."

"Gracie!!!"

She hangs up. Boy, I just can't catch a break.

Chapter 11

DRAKE

I couldn't believe what I was seeing – Sadie, carrying and kissing the baby. Where the heck is the nurse? I yank the baby from her arms.

"NO!" Sadie yells. "Please don't take her away from me."

I tell the nurse not to let Sadie see the baby again because she's been adopted.

"Please, Drake, don't take her away from me," Sadie sobs for her baby. "Bonnie is mine, why are you doing this to me?"

THE STORY OF SADIE FOX

"You can't name her, Sadie, she's not yours anymore." Pulling her hair to make her be quiet, I'm shaking her and slapping her face until she bleeds from her nose. I convince the doctor to take her home and give her a few days to recover before I put her back to work. Then I find out she can't have sexual intercourse for forty days. Fuck that shit! A week, maximum, and she will be back to being my meal ticket.

Sadie cries for days. The bitch just won't be quiet. What's a guy to do? She's a horrible mess and I have to get her in top shape.

*   *   *

SADIE

Lying on the bed, with no hope in sight. I haven't bathed for days. What the fudge is wrong with me? I'm bleeding so much and he wants me to have sex with those nasty men after fighting with him that he had to wait for forty days.

Blue called me to see how I was, but Drake made me hang up. He told me Cal was having a baby and my tears descend, with no mercy. He found a pretty woman to love. I knew he loved me, but I love that monster that made me into the whore that I am. I'm just damaged goods, having nightmares about my baby, wondering who has her, are they treating her well? Is she crying for me? Every day that goes by, my baby is growing and she will never know I'm her mommy. It hurts so badly.

*   *   *

CALVIN

The moment we were waiting for finally arrives. Gracie is having our baby and we're in the hospital. Her pain is not that bad and I'm staying with her, giving her kisses on her forehead and putting ice chips in her mouth. She pushes five times and we heard our baby crying, we're both tearing up also, with eyes of happiness, but I'm wishing it was mine and Sadie's. "It's a boy, Calvin, and he's the spitting image of his daddy," Gracie tells me.

We kiss, but it just wasn't the same, being with Gracie. My true love is Sadie, but I can't have her and she wants to stay with Drake. She thinks she's in love with him, but he's all she knows because he stole her so young.

"Give me my baby boy, Cal. He is so beautiful. I love you, baby," she coos, kissing his cheeks. "I could've sworn he smiled at me," she giggles. We both laugh.

*   *   *

It was supposed to be my special day, I'm a daddy now. Calling Blue, he was ecstatic, since he will be his godfather when the boy's old enough to be baptized. I've always talked to Blue about the way I felt, but he always told me to move on and stop thinking about Sadie. But that's easier said than done. I felt guilty about having my son while she was yearning for her baby girl. I can't help her, though, I had my own family to worry about, now. We named my son Cooper and he was such a trooper, in every sense of the word. He was my boy and loving him is easy. We were happy, for a while, with my little family. Gracie was a good mom but my thoughts were always with Sadie. He had her drinking and pimping her to all his wicked friends. There was nothing I could do for her, I just needed to focus on my own family.

Chapter 12

DRAKE

Your friend Cal had his baby boy, Sadie. I heard he is so in love with Gracie. Wow, just think, I'm an uncle now. Makes you his aunt, I guess," Drake taunts me.

He likes taunting me. He knew this would make me poignant and sad, so that's why he told me.

"Don't worry, you won't be seeing him much. Gracie doesn't want him near us, like we're losers or something. Well, who gives a heck? I never want to be a daddy, or an uncle, anyway. Calvin won't have time to save you, my precious dove. Go get ready; my buddies want a clean bitch. I'm going to the market, first. There's a sale on beer and the way you're drinking, I've got to stock up."

*   *   *

SADIE

The guys are playing poker and I'm watching from the red room. Drake thought it would be awesome to put a red light bulb in and named it the red room. He should have named it the sex room! I turn twenty-one on Saturday and have been his meal ticket for five years now. He uses me and abuses me in every possible way. Sometimes I wish to run away, but the fear gets in the way. A phobia that no one would love me or care for me. I have been dependent on him since he took me that very first night. It was my first and last date with any guy. He stole my innocence that night and he trained me to be a nasty girl. He was a terrible poker player and lost every single time, but I paid the price. I'm still young, although my body feels so old. I didn't have a normal life, I never went to my prom, or graduated middle school or high school. Drake was a con man, a manipulator who preys on young girls. One day he will throw me out when he no longer has any use for me.

That will be my biggest nightmare. For now, I'm just going to fill my addictions – my drinking and my sex problem. Drake loses the poker game – no surprise there – and the guy with a grey suit comes to me. He's tall, with short blond hair and piercing green eyes.

"You're mine for the night, baby," he tells me.

The way he speaks is sexy. Everything about him was a mystery and he had my attention with his sexy smile and with those dimples – he was making me so wet.

Drake yells at me, "He has you for the night. Go with him, he'll be bringing you back tomorrow."

"My name is Craig," he tells me. "Come on, Sadie, my driver is waiting for us."

I go with him, holding his hand. His driver opens the limousine door and off we go. I was feeling self-conscious, dressed like a slut, and he was such a good-looking guy, so clean-cut.

*   *   *

He puts his fingers inside my muff. "Well, young lady, you are very wet. Do I turn you on? Answer me!" he shouts.

"Yes!"

"That's good, baby. You will like what I do to you. It will make you have multiple orgasms. Go take a bubble bath, baby, Kim will show you to your room," he tells me.

THE STORY OF SADIE FOX

I take a hot bath, with candles all over, dim lights, drinking Champagne – Dom Perignon 2006 Vintage, no less. I only know that because Kim lifts the bottle and I can read the label. It tastes different from the cheap six-pack of beer. When walking to my room for the night, I'm wearing a sheer mesh see-through slip. It's really short, so my butt cheeks are showing. My blonde hair was straight and long, past my waist, and my white six-inch heels were so sexy; I felt sexy. He was standing in his room, by his king-sized bed. His bedroom was exquisite and he was gorgeous. Craig, hair all wet and messy, his body is solid, just wearing silk boxers. He licks his lips in anticipation.

"You look beautiful, Sadie, your papilla are so hard, like pearl pebbles." He kisses me greedily and his tongue touches my tonsils – so deep. He pinches my nipples rigid and my moans are loud. He carries me to the bed and I leave the heels on the floor before he starts thrashing my love button like no other.

"I like your bare pussy, sweetie," he whispers. "You have a body that men would give the world for, so what are you doing with a loser like Drake?"

Of course, I don't say anything. Drake is my husband, after all. Craig Baxter is on top of me, biting gently on my nipples, giving each one his attention. Kissing my neck, he takes his time, kissing and teasing every inch of my body. He was driving me crazy. I love this kind of sex. Calvin had sex with me this way, so tenderly licking my sweet spot – it was amazing, my eyes are closed so tightly, enjoying this wonderful feeling. He told me while he was touching my muffin, I should feel myself. I had two orgasms and then many more, later that night.

Chapter 13

SADIE

I was back in the old, wicked clutches of Drake's games of drinking and sex entertainment, with sex games and lots of men touching me every which way they could. There was no break in sight and my hunger for sex was becoming enormous. Drake had made me this way and now I needed it so badly I would fuck the postman, the UPS guy, even the gardener. They all wanted my sexual favors after they feed my addiction, fucking me roughly. I'm a nasty, nasty girl now, with my drinking and my sex addiction. Who would ever want me? Suddenly, life has no meaning for me and Drake's mind games and evil tricks have been working on me for years. I can't leave him, he has me in his web of lustful sex acts – mind games that drive me insane. For once, I wish he could just win, but he's a terrible poker player, so I always end up with these dirty men who smell. Their hygiene is horrible. In desperation, I call Calvin.

"Hi, Calvin, could you come over? I would like a tattoo."

"Sure, sweetie, be there soon," he replies.

Calvin comes at high speed. Hearing his Harley-Davidson and the roar of the motor gives me a thrill. My friend is here and all of a sudden, my heart starts to skip a beat. Cal hugs me and gives me a kiss on the cheek.

"Hi, sweetie, how you doing?" he asks.

"I'm fine, Cal. I just felt like getting a tattoo done."

"Where would you like it?"

"On my arm, please," I tell him.

He organizes his machine and needles. He is a professional tattoo artist and after he puts all the equipment on the table, he sterilizes every piece.

"Sadie, this is going to hurt." I nod, before he adds, "What would you like on your arm?"

"I would like some flowers."

"What kind of flowers?"

"Wildflowers," is all I can think of.

He just draws free-hand on my arm. He was not kidding; the pain was unpleasant but bearable.

Calvin finally finished and it was absolutely beautiful.

"You like it?" he inquired.

"Yes! You are a true artist and it was worth the pain. I love it!"

"I'm glad, Sadie, it's one of my best works ever."

*   *   *

CALVIN

Sadie hugs me and gives me a huge kiss. How I love this girl, my heart is going into over-drive and I want to throw her against the wall, fall into her arms, and shower her with the love that's been festering through my veins for so long – the want that hurts, not to have the one you love with you.

We decide we want to go for a burger. "Let's go to Tommy Burger," I suggest. We were on cloud nine, especially since we were famished. It was like old times, spending time with her.

"Sadie, I'm a daddy now and I have a girl-friend. We fight constantly, but thank God my job takes me away from her jealousy. She knows I love you, Sadie, there's no denying it any longer," I blurt out to her.

"How is your son, Cal?" is all she asks.

"He's wonderful, he's the love of my life,

Chapter 14

CALVIN

I called your work, Cal, where were you? I'm leaving you. I always could tell when you'd been with her. You smell like her. It has always been Sadie, hasn't it? Where is the suitcase, Cal?"

"It's in the closet. Why are you doing this, Gracie?"

"You have a lot of fucking nerve asking me that, Cal. I'm taking Cooper and moving in with my mother until we can get our own place."

Grabbing her arm, I warn her, "You are not taking my son from me."

"Just watch me, asshole."

"Let's not do this, Gracie, please," I beg.

"Don't worry, you'll still see Cooper. I would never take him away from you – just as long as you pay your child support, you won't have a problem."

"Daddy," Cooper squeals, as he runs into my arms.

I kiss him and give him a huge hug. "You be a good boy, big guy, and take care of your mommy." He's only three and it's breaking my heart that I won't see him every day. Tears flow and I wipe my eyes. Gracie is leaving me and I didn't even sleep with Sadie – only one kiss. I guess it is cheating, in a dishonest kind of way, but what's done is done. Why cry over spilled milk? Life goes on.

"'Bye, Calvin. I hope one day you will stop loving her, so you can get on with life. You are a perfect dad."

We kiss and hold each other, for a while. We will always be connected through our precious son.

"Don't go to your mom's house, Gracie. I'll buy you a two-bedroom house, with a yard, so Cooper can run and play with his toys."

*   *   *

We were busy at work; all the twenty-one-year-old girls wanted a tattoo of a Tiffany chain anklet with a heart. They looked real and I was grateful for the work.

"Hey, Cal, I heard about Gracie," Blue started.

"Don't want to talk about it, Blue."

"Well, I'm here if you need me."

"Thanks, dude," was all I could reply.

We take a coffee break – I needed my caffeine fix.

"Did you hear Drake is having a huge party?" Blue asked me. "Hey! I heard they will have a poker game and orgies – that he's planning to auction off Sadie to the highest bidder."

"That son-of-a-bitch, will it never end? Why does he have to hurt her at every party? One day I will beat him to a pulp and get some guys to fuck his ass so hard that he won't be able to move or walk."

"That, my friend, could definitely be arranged," Blue offered.

We both laugh – it was just a thought, but a bloody good thought.

*   *   *

DRAKE

The party is bumping and the poker game is starting. It's all high-stakes tonight. I go to Sadie and tell her to drink some beer.

"Okay," she replies.

"Do it now, because whoever wins, will have you all the way through till Sunday."

THE STORY OF SADIE FOX

Sadie looks hot, wearing a sexy white mini-skirt, a very slutty red G-string, and a red mesh transparent blouse with no bra, and I want her to be in a sexy mood. Holy fuck! Her breasts are huge and she's already drinking her beer. I paid for some strippers, also – some that will do special favors for money. The dudes love all this attention from sexy women. Placing my money on the table to play poker, Craig, Dan, Jack, and I are playing when the door slams open, hitting the wall. Calvin and Blue, that gay boyfriend of his, walk in like they own my place – stupid jerks!

*   *   *

CALVIN

I laugh at Drake's face. His expression is priceless. The guy that got my attention, though, was the guy with the grey suit and black silk tie. I'd never seen him before. Turning to the red door where Sadie fucks all the jerks, she's standing there and her beauty speaks for itself. I'm wanting her badly, so we all have a seat. I'm trying to win Sadie for the night. Blue kicks my leg to calm me down, but I can't help it.

Sadly, I didn't win the poker game – that guy in the grey suit did. He has a grin that I hate, especially since I know he'll get to touch her and devour every inch of her body, taste her sugary lips. She's happy he won the game. Wow, she likes this guy. She never even smiled at me as he put his coat on her and they leave. What the hell?

Chapter 13

CRAIG

You seem happy that I won, my sexy lover. You are a beauty, Sadie," I tell her.

"Well, you know how to treat a woman, Craig. I like the way you touch me and I'm so horny. Craig, take me here and now. Make love to me roughly and give me deep kisses."

Pushing her against the wall, I bite her nipples hard, swirling my tongue. She zips down my zipper, all so seductively, and my cock is huge. She gets to her knees and with her full, luscious lips parted her tongue, inch by inch, licks the tip of the head of my penis with lustful hunger. She sucks, stroking and provoking it to get bigger. She's asking for it, so I take my hardness between her legs, pumping her sweet spot. I hold her firm ass. Having sex with her is an absolute delight. Her nipples swell in my mouth as her moans become erratic – the cries of her sexual pleasure were truly a treasure.

I couldn't stop touching her – she was groaning in my ear, biting my chin as she yelled with pleasure. We had sexy games, along with toys, all night long and we prolonged our sexual bliss with a thrill. We turn off the lights, having sexual pleasure one more time. We loved having sex together, as we both had a powerful need for enjoyment. I wish could buy her – for a heavy price, knowing Drake the way I do. He won't let me have her, I'm sure, so I'll just take whatever I can get.

"Craig, that was wonderful, baby. You always fulfill my every sexual need and we're great together." Wanting more, we are addicted to lust and sex, she hugs me. I'm not used to that kind of affection, but liking her was an understatement. We will be together again.

*   *   *

CALVIN

We leave the poker game and go to a sports bar, where we have some shots and a couple of beers.

"I know you're disappointed you didn't win Sadie. That dude that won her is at least fond of her and she's with money," Blue consoles me.

"But I love her, body and soul, Blue. She's the only one who could make me whole. I tried to love someone and make a family with her but everything went wrong and it's because of my love for Sadie. Let me have another four shots, I'm going to get fucked up tonight."

"You can't just drown your sorrows, Cal. You

just have to suck it up, life goes on, my friend."

"That's easy for you to say, you've found the love of your life."

"Yes, that's true, I have Ken and he's a dream come true. I don't underestimate fate, though, he could leave me for someone else tomorrow. Who knows? Life can be great and it can be cruel."

"That's the truth," is all I can offer.

"I have something to tell you, Cal."

"What is it, Blue? I hope it's some great news. More drinks, please!"

"Ken and I are getting married. We're going to San Francisco and I want you to be my best man."

"Wow!" I'm almost speechless. "I'm honored to be your best man, congrats, bro."

Hugs and then more drinking follow.

"We have to celebrate," I enthuse. "We will make it a weekend you will never forget."

We spend the night drinking, talking, and planning. It will be a gay wedding like no other. At some point, Ken came to join the celebration and we all had a fantastic time – our friendship was real and important. I was happy for Blue; he's gone through so much. His parents don't accept him because he's gay, he was bullied in school and got beaten up on numerous occasions for his sexuality; unlike Ken, whose family loves him. It's true what they say – love is blind and opposites attract.

Chapter 16

SADIE

Craig lavishes me with lovely gifts and gives enough money to Drake for his poker games so I could spend the weekend with him. We have a blast – we would role play and he'd blindfold me. It is so delicious that when it's time to go home it saddens me because it felt normal with him. Drake just used me and I was getting tired of his ways, but I was too weak to leave.

Drake was bringing another young girl and showing her the ropes, just the way he did me. Was he getting rid of me? That was my biggest fear. Fear and fear alone could kill you. I was not that young, sweet sixteen-year-old anymore or even a vivacious girl. I have never worked a real job in my life, so what do I put in my resumé as my experience? I have sex with my husband's friends – achievements: sex for a six-pack.

I do have a skill. I know how to drink and how to give blowjobs. They will think I'm a whore and it will all be true. Tears start sliding down my cheeks and an overwhelming anxiety overtakes me. My body starts to shiver. I don't have any ambitions; Drake took everything from me and now he will throw me away like a piece of trash. I'm scared, and staring at the mirror I realize I've already developed dark rings under my eyes and my face is so pale. I'm only twenty-four and yet I feel like I'm forty-four. That's the reason he is going to get rid of me. Running to my bed, with tears of anxiety flowing. There's a puddle on my pillow. Falling asleep would come later in the night, along with dreams of loneliness.

*　　*　　*

BLUE

We all flew to San Francisco for the wedding and we're all staying in a hotel.

"Blue, are you happy?" Ken asks me. "I love you so much and we will share our lives together, forever!"

"Ken, I've waited my whole life for you. Being gay, it hasn't been easy and it's nice to finally find a soul-mate to share my life with."

"Blue, thank you for making my dreams come true."

Being on a cruise on San Francisco Bay while we get married, everything will be unforgettable and ridiculously gorgeous. "Come here, Ken, let me kiss those thick, juicy lips."

Our muscular tongues are tasting, caressing, like a luscious song; every lick with sweet tongues, with such rhythm. "I want you here and now," I demand.

"Wait until the honeymoon, Blue Steel," Ken chuckles.

"I can't help it. I've waited all my life for you, Ken. Let me love you in the shower, baby."

"Will you stop touching my cock. You will wait, Mr. Blue Steel."

"Let me hold you tightly. I will love you for the rest of my life."

"I feel the same way," Ken remarks, hoarse with emotion.

We're two muscular men standing with black tuxedos on; two beautiful hearts beating as one and staring at one another with love, passion, lust, and friendship – the whole package – that will soon be united for life.

I got down on my knees. I just couldn't help myself or wait any longer.

Unbuckling Ken's belt, he says, "I told you to wait."

MARTHA PEREZ

"Do you really want to wait, baby?"

We both laugh and I pull out his long length of thick, rigid pole and fill my mouth with its splendor. With long licks and sucking, with so much anticipation, he moans, which just makes me suck it harder. It drives me crazy when I satisfy my partner.

Chapter 17

KEN

I frown when I see Drake with his group of low-lifes and, to my surprise, Dale Coleman, the worst of the group, was even here. Take that back, Drake is the biggest slimeball, simply by having these guys turn up on my wedding day. This will not go well.

"What are you all doing here?" I demand.

Drake speaks up, "Blue invited Sadie, my wife, and where she goes, I go."

"Well, that's certainly not what I heard," I snap back at him.

"Don't listen to gossip, Ken. Anyways, I didn't even know two men could get married."

Drake laughs. "Get out of my sight, you and your group of filthy bastards, pushing your way into my group of family and friends." I can't stand the sight of them. "The ceremony will begin very soon, so have some champagne, mingle, and thank you all for coming to our special day," I manage to spit out between gritted teeth.

*   *   *

BLUE

The room looks like a magical fairytale. Beautiful lights were twinkling, giving the room a cozy ambience. The red roses, Vera Wang crystal-vase centerpieces, the silk white tablecloths with black napkins, and gold candles create an unsurpassed, romantic atmosphere – nothing could be more beautiful. I'm beside the captain of the ship, waiting for Ken to walk to me. Calvin is my best man and he looks handsome with his tux. He keeps staring at Sadie, though. She was wearing a long silky red dress with her long blonde hair cascading down her shoulders. She is a lovely woman and she looks incredibly classy. Drake was getting mad at her, that asshole always makes a scene, but he won't mess up my wonderful mood or my special day.

Ken walks toward me slowly. Loving this man has been the best thing I ever did. He is so gorgeous. We smile and my heart is thumping with every beat. No, it's not nervousness, this was so meant to be – him and I, our lives together. We hold hands and the ceremony begins and, in the end, without interruptions, "You may kiss." Our lips open, with our tongues dancing a fine rhythm. We both had our white-gold bands on as proof of our love. We turn and Cal is the first one to hug us. He's been a true friend. Drake and his entourage didn't bother to give their congrats, not even a glance our way, but we didn't care. Sadie comes and hugs both of us with her sweet grin and gives her huge red luscious smile to Calvin. We go and take photos on the deck and, after a few hours of drinking champagne, we go downstairs to the reception area. The lights are dim, with a jazz band playing; everyone is mingling.

*   *   *

CALVIN

There was a delicious buffet of seafood and steak, with tasteful desserts. Everything looks exquisite and everyone is enjoying their meal. I'm keeping an eye on Drake as he's been drinking and profusely yanking Sadie's arm. He can't even let her eat. He whispers something in her ear and his buddies just start laughing loudly. He's an imbecile!

I get up. I want to offer a toast. So, with my champagne in hand, I begin. "Blue, you have been my friend since we were ten years old. We were both borderline crazy and that made us like close brothers. Ken, you have been a great friend and wonderful to my best friend. Wishing you both happiness and lots of love. May you be happy forever. Cheers to you both! Everyone – cheers!"

Chapter 18

BLUE

Everything was going fine when I heard a cry of, "Calvin, don't go over there. Drake is her husband."

"That piece of shit, he's hitting her. I'm going to kill that motherfucker."

I run over and grab him.

"Let me go, Blue."

"Okay, Cal," I said, "but take it easy, okay?"

* * *

CALVIN

Drake twists her hair like a ragdoll as he slaps her. My rage wanted to kill him, once and for all. Hearing her weeping made me angrier and filled my veins with hatred. They were next to the cake as I punch him, breaking his nose. When his buddies start to kick me, everything went into slow motion. Dale takes out a Beretta M9 and starts shooting wildly. He hit my leg and, wincing with pain, I move to shield Sadie. Her screams are earsplitting, with bullets flying everywhere and people running all over the place. All I can hear are screams and, when I hear Blue calling Ken's name, I turn.

Blue is holding him, crying, "Don't leave me, please." Ken stares into Blue's eyes.

"Someone call the paramedics. Hurry, for fuck's sake," I shout.

"Don't die on me," Blue sobs, caressing Ken's

face, with tears rolling down his own.

Ken takes a deep breath. He holds Blue's shoulders and with his soft voice he whispers, "I love you, Blue!"

"No, no, no, please don't go." Ken took his last breath as Blue's lips touch his for a final time.

Everyone was eerily silent. Blue puts his face on Ken's chest and my own tears begin to flow down my face. How could this happen? Why?

After they take Ken away, I say to Blue, "Come on, let's go now."

I have to go to the hospital – it just seems like the bullet scraped off the surface layer of my skin.

The police interrogate all of us, asking routine questions. They let us leave and take me to the ER.

"I don't want to leave," Blue sobs, yelling at the family members. They will take him to my place.

He says, "Ken is gone, Cal, the love of my life is gone. I'm going to kill Dale. He messed with the wrong guy. It's your brother's fault, though, he's a loser and they'd better all watch their backs." Those were his last words to me.

*   *   *

DRAKE

"What the hell, Dale? Why did you bring that gun with you? You killed that gay guy. Blue will come after us."

"Let that motherfucker come after me. You know me, I hate gay guys. I'll kill him too."

"You'd better get lost, Dale. He will try to murder you; never underestimate your opponent, fool."

"Shut the fuck up," Dale snaps. "We shouldn't have gone there anyway. I wanted to go to a poker game, but no, you had to listen to that slut of a wife of yours. Well, it's done. We have to know when to fold. Now we have to be ready for the consequences. I want to go fuck some women, now."

"Let's go, then," I offer. "Where is Sadie?"

She was standing with Calvin and he wouldn't let her go.

"What an asshole," I exclaim.

*　　　*　　　*

BLUE

I can't believe what happened today. I'm sitting, drinking a bottle of vodka, just wanting to be by myself and wishing I would get alcohol poisoning. Listening to jazz, I keep drinking, remembering Ken's face when we were getting married, saying our 'I dos,' the plans we had, the honeymoon we were going to in Italy, where we would have stayed for ten days. I can't stop seeing his face. He was scared to die and leave me. My heart is in anguish and my soul is vacant. Throwing the bottle against the wall, the shattered glass was all over the place. Crawling to my bed with tears, I cry out loud – I was falling apart. Dale had destroyed my life. He took the life of a marvelous man and he will pay for that. I can guarantee – an eye for an eye! Killing him will become my goal in life.

Chapter 19

SADIE

I struggle to get out of bed. Calvin is still sleeping on the couch with his leg wrapped up, still wearing his white dress shirt. My dress was covered in blood, and he went to his chest of drawers for a clean shirt for me.

I'm feeling bad about what took place yesterday. Dale is a ruthless man. He got Dottie hooked on drugs, threw her out onto the street, and now she has sex just to get her fix. If I know Blue, he will go after him.

What about my predicament? Drake is with

that sixteen-year-old bitch and has pushed me aside. Soon I'll be on the street, with Dottie, doing men like a real prostitute. Making breakfast with my thoughts of hell; it's been a long night. I'm hungry and Cal will be too. I start cleaning the mess of his room and washing his clothes. Guys are so messy and it's the least I can do for him.

*   *   *

CALVIN

Smelling bacon wakes me up, loving that Sadie has taken the initiative to be comfortable and to make breakfast. I'm wondering how Blue is feeling in the aftermath of the tragedy and sorrow, for all of us. I don't know how Blue will get on. We all will miss Ken. I have to help him with the funeral arrangements. Ken wanted to be cremated, he told Blue one night when we were drinking. I will pay for all the services. Blue is my bro and he's been there with me for the good, the bad, and the ugly. I'll do anything for him.

I take a seat and eat my breakfast. Sadie was taking a shower as I was reading the newspaper. "The Wedding of the Century Ends in Tragedy," blares at me from the headline.

*   *   *

I turn the key to Blue's house and when I walk in it stinks of liquor. He'd drunk all night and bottles were everywhere. When I find Blue, he is on his bed in a not-so-comfortable curved position. I really don't want to wake him up, so I just took a seat, watching him. Taking Sadie home had made me feel indignant. Drake will punish her.

I'm going to get an ulcer if I keep continuing this insanity of worrying about someone that I can't love or save. Chewing my toothpick, my thoughts are always of Sadie now. Thinking of

THE STORY OF SADIE FOX

Blue, though, his wounded heart is my despair. He's my best friend and running my hand through my hair, with my head down, I finally get up and start to make myself useful by cleaning all the mess. Hearing the shower, I realize he's up now, for all the sadness of his life.

We make the arrangements for the funeral, order the flowers, and where his ashes will be placed for his final resting place. It's difficult. Blue didn't say a word but tears are running down his face the whole time. My heart hurt for him. He's like a zombie, walking with no faith. It's a gloomy day of despair, with the skies teeming with grey clouds. They only move in for this day; yesterday it was the clearest of days, and it was sunny and beautiful. Today will end in a befitting downpour, washing all our tears away. With the storm coming our way, we will have to wait for another day. They say time heals all wounds. Only time will tell, for Blue.

"Come on, Blue, stay with me," I tell him.

MARTHA PEREZ

He walks with his head down, not caring about what I say... like a puppy in the cold, with no food. He's a man with no hope, his dreams of happiness are gone. We drink the night away, as I take care of my best friend.

Chapter 20

SADIE

D rake is sleeping with Desiree Parker. She's the new girl, only sixteen. He gives me all the nasty men, most of the time, and I was just having sex constantly. My room had become the red-light special. At this point, I was drinking a six-pack twice a day, as I couldn't stand the pain of my body. Sometimes, I was fucking up to seven times a day, with no food, maybe eating once a day and no breaks. At times, he throws me a turkey sandwich, which I devour, and guzzle the water before my tricks came to play their nasty web of games. I'm tired of my life. It's all I knew and I'm jealous of Drake's new girl. I hear them having sex, knowing full well he is about to throw me out like an old shoe. I'm simply scared of the unknown.

The talk on the street is that Blue is going after Dale. He will get even. He's not the same anymore. No longer in the game of life. He's depressed and drinking all day, every day.

Drake is up to something. He's being very secretive and it scares me. I heard Dottie was found in a motel, raped and stabbed twenty-one times. My heart breaks for her. We were two friends with dreams who met the wrong guys; well, fully-grown men actually, taking young girls to pay their poker debts. Time goes by faster than the wind can blow you away and then that awful night came when Drake told me three men had paid him for me.

"All three will have sex with you, Sadie, and you'd better let them."

THE STORY OF SADIE FOX

My tears were streaming down my cheeks as I screamed at him, "I won't do it, Drake. I'm tired of being your nasty little sex toy!"

"What did you say? You are my bitch! You're going to do it and, by the way, we are divorced."

My mouth falls to the floor.

"This will be your last night, Sadie. I married Desiree and she's having my baby. So, after you finish your gang-bang tonight, pack your bags and get out. My wife hates you and doesn't want to see the sight of you again."

"Drake, how could you do this to me?" I scream at him.

"It is what it is, baby. That's life. Your cake's done here."

"Why are you having a baby? You sold my baby girl because I loved her."

"I didn't love you, though. Did I, bitch?" he snarls. "Using you was my pleasure and I've got to admit, you took me out of a lot of outstanding debts."

173

"I'm not a dog you can just throw away, Drake."

"Just watch me," he chuckles. He gives me a kiss on my cheek with a smirk on his lips. "You're wasted, Sadie, all used up. You're not that sixteen-year-old guys wanted anymore. They want young fish on their dish and you just don't cut it."

Tears descend slowly. He's right, I'm damaged goods and, feeling sorry for myself, I get dressed.

*   *   *

Three huge guys were waiting in the red room. I know this is going to be brutal when one of the guys pull my hair and bites my chin. I scream, so he slaps my face.

"Remove your clothes," he commands, with a rough voice. "You will be so fucked up!"

Removing my clothes, I was not fast enough for them and the other guy handcuffs me to the bedpost. He removes the rest of my clothes until I am totally nude; all three men were ruthless.

Taking a deep breath, I wait as they blindfold me. One of the men bit my arms and legs, making me cry out, it hurt so badly. He did it with no compunction; he was just a sadistic bastard. The other man whips me as tears pour down my face. One stuck his fingers in my mouth and I bit them with all my might. He hit me so hard, I almost passed out. I could smell cigarette smoke and I screamed bloody murder as my skin was burning and the pain was throbbing. I toss and turn, pulling the handcuffs even tighter, so they were cutting into my wrists.

Chapter 21

CALVIN

I thought my heart would break in half when I got that phone call that Sadie was in the hospital. They didn't give me any details and my heart was beating rapidly, my throat was tightening, my chest was tightly wound, in pain. Walking into the room, everything was white, smelling like cleaning products. She looks small in the bed, so fragile; she's black and blue. This can't be true. I'm in total disbelief that Drake could have let this happen. I'm going to kill that pathetic slimeball. My toothpick breaks in half from clenching my jaw in anger. I ask the nurse if I can be alone with her. She nods.

Sadie's face was purple, with black outlines. As I was checking her, I realize her nipples had been bitten and my tears fell to the sheets. So many bites and deep scratches, I couldn't bear to look any longer. I put the sheets back, covering her.

"Calvin," she murmurs. "Calvin, where are you?"

Grabbing her hand, I whisper, "I'm right here, baby-doll."

"My body hurts," she whimpers.

"You'll be fine, Sadie. Don't move, honey." They burned her with cigarettes butts – she will be scarred for life. She will never be the same. After they were done with her, Drake had thrown her out on the street. Fortunately, a good Samaritan called the ambulance and they brought her to the emergency department.

When I get my hands on Drake, he'll be so

sorry he did this to her. I should let Blue kill him, but he's not worth going to jail for the rest of our lives. Thank God they didn't burn her face, but they did burn her breasts, stomach, and legs. She has marks all over and the doctors had to do a hysterectomy. They removed her uterus, so she can never have any more children. Maybe that will be for the best. She is so damaged, but I will be there for her. She's my love, my life.

After two weeks I take her home and she surprises me.

"Calvin, I want my own apartment."

"Why would you want to be by yourself?" I ask.

"Because I want to be alone, Cal. Please, I'm begging you!"

"I don't like it," I tell her, "but, okay, baby-doll. I'll find you an apartment."

She's wearing an all-black ensemble; all covered, no makeup, and she walks slowly with her head down, always sitting on the couch, watching television, no life left in her. She doesn't even turn when I speak to her. I can't blame her – my brother has destroyed this woman. I buy her a condo in the next block from my house because I wanted to be close to her, to take care of her and to try to make her normal again. I'll die trying.

I've got to talk to Blue, got to make a plan to ruin Drake's life eternally. Not kill him, but to disfigure and injure him, with no repair in sight. He may be my brother, but only by my father fucking around. A sadistic bastard he was too. Those two have the blood of the devil. My mom was kind-hearted, but we never knew what happened to her. Mila Fox disappeared. No one knows anything about where she's gone. She was with my dad, but they never found her body, or her, for that matter. I talk to Blue about our plan and he agrees.

"Hell yeah!" It's the first time he came alive since Ken's passing.

MARTHA PEREZ

I furnish the condo, buying her a forty-inch flat screen TV, mounting it on the wall; a comfy brown recliner; and pictures of roses all over her walls. Everywhere, I put pictures of flowers. But I'm scared since she doesn't even want to go outside, again, but closed herself off in the condo. Maybe she should talk to a therapist. All of Sadie's scars I will tattoo over to cover them. So people won't notice them and she'll feel beautiful again.

Chapter 22

CALVIN

"Hi, Cal, the plan is in place," Blue informs me.

"Okay, Blue."

It's Friday and Blue tells his friends that he was having a poker game with lots of money involved; fifty thousand dollars, in fact. We make sure Dale and Drake finds out, since this game is underground. There is a full moon and Blue's friends are all drinking, laughing, having fun. Before the plan is set in motion, I make sure Sadie is comfy at the condo. Drake will never know where she lives.

We're in the other room, watching. We don't want Dale or Drake to know this is an ambush.

"Blue, what are you going to do to Dale?" I query.

"Don't ask, Cal, you won't approve."

"I really don't give a shit, Blue. They deserve everything they are getting."

As we watch them playing poker, Drake is drinking masses of beer. I don't want him drunk because I want him to feel every ounce of pain that the guys have planned for him. We're under-ground and it's sound-proof here.

* * *

DALE

"Stop smoking weed, Dale, you'll smell the room up," Drake tells me.

"What the heck, Drake! Stop nagging and give me another beer. Just because you wear those fancy suits doesn't give you the ticket to treat me like a waiter. Just shuffle the cards already," I snap back at him.

I check my cards and Drake gives me the eye. I hide a card and slip out another.

The guys know what they were doing, but they don't care. They are not getting any money, that's for sure. The game gets intense with more in the pot. Drake is grinning from ear-to-ear. He yells, "I win... I win." He grabs the money toward him when the biker guy takes his knife out. Drake says, "Hey man, I won".

"You are a huge cheater," Biker Guy drawls. He puts the knife against Drake's neck, deeper.

"Hey, what are you doing, man!" Drake protests.

"You'll see, now sit your ass down and we will tell you what this is all about."

183

The guys are laughing, mostly at Drake, because he is kind of drunk and looks confused. These guys are determined to scare Drake and me, but I'm fearless and they'd better kill me because, whatever they do, my rage is building up. I'll kill every single one of them. My fists are busting to kick their asses.

"What are we waiting for?" I ask.

"Shut that mouth up," the biker dude warns me, "or I'll shut your trap up permanently. Do you want your last beer? You'd better enjoy it, because life as you know it is over."

We take the beer.

*　　*　　*

CALVIN

Ready to kick some ass. I'm ready as we walk into the room. Drake's face is priceless, the fear evident. Dale, on the other hand, is an asshole who doesn't care what the fuck happens. He's such an evil person, a heartless beast, but he'll be in hell soon, burning for all his sins. Blue takes Dale to one of the rooms – it was soundproof.

*   *   *

BLUE

"I hope you're ready for this beating, because I won't stop until you're a dead piece of shit."

We start boxing, letting him warm up one-on-one, fair and square. We start punching and I let him hit me a couple of times. Hitting Dale is an absolute pleasure. He killed Ken, the love of my life. All I can feel is rage as I beat and pound him mercilessly. Already black, blue, and purple, his face swells but I continue to hammer him with no interruptions. He finally falls to the floor, where I just carry on kicking him until he doesn't move anymore. I bend down to take his pulse – he's dead.

Chapter 23

CALVIN

I go home with my hands clean. My son and Sadie need me and I can't risk going to jail. I let Blue's friends do the thrashing and ass-whipping. I can still hear Drake saying, "Calvin, don't leave me here with these guys."

They're all muscular, handsome, and gay. I told all five of them to fuck him until he can't take it anymore, to beat him until he can't walk. Grinning as I'm walking away, I hear him yell, "Calvin!"

I ignore his screams. He may be my brother, but I will never forgive Drake for what he did to

Sadie. He damaged that girl and sold her body. She had dreams at sixteen. I still remember the first time my eyes connected with hers.

Passing by her condo on my way home, I notice the television is on, no lights, just the luminous gleam of light from the TV. My heart skips a beat, worrying about her. But at least she's safe now.

*   *   *

There's a knock at the door. My hair is messy and my breath smells of cognac. I save the high-quality stuff, from western France, for special occasions. The knock is louder this time.

"Alright, I'm coming. Hold on."

When I open the door, I'm greeted by, "Hi, Cal!"

"Hey, Blue."

"I've got some news about your brother and Dale."

THE STORY OF SADIE FOX

"Do I need another drink?"

"You and me both, dude," Blue chuckles.

We have a shot of tequila each. "Cheers!"

We swallow the burning liquid quickly. I wipe my mouth with the palm of my hand. We go to the living room.

"Have a seat, Blue, and begin," I urge him.

"You know I had to kill Dale, right? He was just an evil snake."

"Of course! I knew you would waste that maggot. I don't blame, or judge you, bro."

"I know, Cal. You're my best friend and we don't keep secrets. Your brother is in the hospital. He is still alive, but my friends gang-fucked his ass and it was really bad. He's unrecognizable – he's hanging on by a thread."

*   *   *

"Can I see my brother?" I asked.

The nurse answers, "Yes, you can."

"What happened to him?" I wonder, innocently.

"I'll let the doctor talk to you. He will be here at ten."

"Thanks, nurse Janice." She gives me a huge smile and I take a seat, staring at Drake. I have no feelings for him. I don't even feel sorry for him. He deserved whatever he got. I want him to suffer. He's had this coming for a long time. His face is like a monster and his legs are broken, so are his arms. He looks like a mummy. The doctor startles my thoughts as he enters.

"Good morning, Doc," I say.

"Who are you?" he asks suspiciously.

"My name is Calvin. I'm his brother."

"Do you know what happened to your brother?" he inquires.

"No."

"Well, what the police are saying is that he was with the wrong crew. Was he gay?"

"I wouldn't know, Doctor, we are not close

siblings. If he is, he hid it very well. I heard he was having a baby. From time to time, we would catch up with each other in our busy lives. That was the story the last time I talked to him, him telling me about the baby."

*   *   *

I tell the police the same story, letting them know he always plays poker for serious money. I act like the loving brother, putting my fake face on, as I didn't want to give anything away about my friends' involvement. They are depending on me to play my part in this. It is a brother's betrayal at its very worst, but it has to be done. The police are satisfied with my answers and I leave the hospital for my job.

Tiger's Den is busy but my thoughts are with Sadie, biting on my toothpick and thinking what else I can do next for my baby-doll? I have to find out how to take her outside. She's always in the dark and that worries me. It hurts me that she will never again be that vivacious girl I once knew.

EPILOGUE

CALVIN

I check in on my brother, Drake, and discover that he has no feeling in his legs and is now a paraplegic. His wife-to-be has left him. She's young, but she took what little money he had. I paid for his house and bills. The parties still go on. In Drake's world, being in a wheelchair, you might think he would stop the madness, but no, not him. He makes money playing poker, sucking off cunts until the morning light, all the way to the dark of night.

Blue met a nice guy and they are dating. He will never forget Ken, the love of his life, but we do have to go on and try to find happiness. He got his revenge and murdered Dale. Blue will always be my best friend, my right-hand brother – I'll be loving this guy until the day I die.

*   *   *

SADIE

Staring at myself in the mirror, I realize I look older. When staring at my tattoos, underneath were cigarette burns and I choke up. I can't control my cries as my last teardrops fall. Being torn and shattered, it doesn't matter how I hide my scars. I wear them every minute of every day. After putting my jeans and pink sweater on, some black boots, and tying my hair in a ponytail, I take a seat on my comfy recliner. My fears, with my tears, sneak into my mind, body, and soul.

Calvin is knocking on the door. I'm scared, but I open the door.

"Hi, Cal!"

"Hello, baby-doll, can I come in?"

"Sure."

"You look beautiful," he says.

*   *   *

CALVIN

She's staring at me, wearing my jeans, a black cotton t-shirt, flexing my muscles. Her cheeks get all rosy. She's still my girl, my innocent little baby. She turns her head and my grin gets wider.

"Sadie, you like what you see?" I smile. I go toward her and touch her face, giving her a kiss on her forehead. She's turning red and it makes my heart crumble. All I want to do is tumble into bed with her, or even here, on the floor.

"Are you ready to go?" I ask.

"Cal, I'm scared. I can't be with crowds. My fear is making me agoraphobic and I'm going to have a panic attack."

"It's okay, baby. I've got you forever. Fight the fears and don't let them overtake you. Now, breathe deeply. I love you, Sadie Fox, you are my girl."

With her shaky legs, she holds my hand. Her soft hand was so sweet to behold, squeezing so tightly, it almost stops my circulation. I didn't care, her smile is all I need to test her limits.

"You can do this, baby-doll. Come on, walk slowly."

This will be the beginning of our life if she walks out this door.

"Cal, don't let go of my hand," she begs. She's trembling, like a small, little girl. We finally make it outside and she takes in the breeze, deep into her lungs. Her tears fall but I lick them away. We continue to our destination.

"I have a surprise for you," I tell her, as we sit in my black Corvette.

Passing the freeway, I put on some soft rock music.

We made it to our destination without complications. She looks out and she says, "You brought me to the beach."

"Yes, I made a basket of food, winc, and fruit for my baby girl."

Seeing her blue-diamond eyes water, I smile softly.

"I love the ocean, Calvin."

"Come on," I implore her. I can still see the sunset and the moonlight shine on that beautiful face of hers. She smiles. Sadie is still fearful but she's fighting her fears. Taking her to a place she loved was the right thing to do. Blue told me to do it and he was correct.

Laying the soft blanket and food basket down, we lie there talking about little things, drinking wine and, after we had our dinner, she leaned on my chest.

"Look, Cal, the sunset!" she exclaims excitedly.

"Yes, baby-doll, it's lovely, just like you." That was the truth. "Sadie Fox, can I make love to you?" She tenses up, but we start to kiss passionately, our lips connecting and soon it was heated. My penis stirs and I lay her in front of me, the light of the moonlight shining on her beautiful features. I can't stop myself as we bite each other's lips, licking her neckline, sucking her nipples, then blowing on them. They're hardening with my licking. Her moans were so soft, it made me pinch her nipples.

She calls my name, "Cal."

I can't stop, but I ask, "You want me to stop?"

"Hell, no!" she cries back. We both laugh with joy.

Going down to her muff, my tongue goes wild. Then going to her navel with my tongue ring, her metal ring, it was wild and out of this world. I was back to thrashing her muffin and she yelled with pleasure. She has an incredibly intense orgasm before she gets on her knees, sucking and licking my cock, to wonderland and beyond.

"Yes, baby, deeper," I moan. I hold her head toward my dick, the sensation is overwhelming as she rocks my world and all my dreams come true. I cum deep in her mouth and she licks me clean. We hold each other, just watching the moonlight. I turn to Sadie.

"Sadie, I love you so much. Will you marry me?"

She kisses me. "Yes, Cal, I would love to spend the rest of my life with you." We hold each other for dear life. Who says dreams don't come true?

We married.

Sadie is now my wife and she works with me. She learned how to tattoo, went to school and became a tattoo artist. My son adores Sadie and we take him on summer vacations. Maybe she doesn't love me like she did Drake, but I try not to think about that. She chose me second. I loved her too much to care. Life is too short and I can't complain. Sadie's mom forgave her – they have a nice relationship now. Her mom couldn't forgive herself for signing those papers, giving Sadie to Drake. Life goes on – we leave the ugly in the past and walk forward to a blissful life.

We are as close to the perfect couple as we can be. I thank God, every day, for second chances.

We lock up Tiger's Den, and holding hands, kissing, our tongues dancing, we are soulmates to the end.

Notes from the Author

"I'm the kind of woman that always likes to smile even when I don't have anything to smile about. I've fallen twice, and each time been able to rise from the ashes and stand tall. When life is at its worst, you must still see the beauty all around you; the birds, roses, mountains, and trees. Then you look back and realize how strong and resilient you really are. The solitude and mere existence have broken my spirit, but my heart has spoken the truth. I go to sleep, toss and turn in disbelief, and hear a voice... 'Darling, you're here to stay with me. I found you lost in the abyss.' That gets me pissed because the only thing I know is that I exist!?"

"The worst pain is when your heart is broken in so many fragments. So tough to mend, but no matter how hearts bleed... they blend with raindrops of tears in the end."

"Will you pick me up with joy or will you turn and let me go and move on, never looking back at what we had and be mad and look elsewhere... or be alone? We have a bond that we can't let go... or was it all a dream?"

"I have made mistakes and paid the price for so many failures. So sue me, I am human just like you. I've learned the hard way that this life gives so many chances, and so much sadness, kindness... and the sorrow that life has to offer. But I still smile."

"Life is short. A beginning of a new day. I will break the rules and refuse to have regrets. So many possibilities... life goes on... I can't wait for my next adventure. Forget yesterday, I'm ready for a new day. I will laugh, smile, dance, and walk away from all the drama and stress. Life is good."

"I'm broken. So many people have taken from me... my body and soul. After what they did to my heart, you may ask why my love is still tough; when I scream at night, smile when it's light, but behind it all, I'm just me with all my baggage... in a cage in my mind. But soon, I'll find the little girl in me and be free."

About the Author

Martha Perez was born in raised in Los Angeles, CA. She now lives in West Covina, CA with her husband Sal Andalon and their dog Sugar Bear. Her hobbies include reading, writing, exercise and going on long walks.

Broken Pieces is her first book, and is an accomplishment of which she is very proud.